Lifelong romance
New Zealand. Wri
with happy ending
create. You can fol
facebook.com/jcha   jcharroway
and twitter.com/jcharroway.

If you liked *A Week to be Wild*, why not try

Off Limits by Clare Connelly
Legal Seduction by Lisa Childs
Ruled by Anne Marsh

Discover more at millsandboon.co.uk.

A WEEK TO BE WILD

JC HARROWAY

MILLS & BOON

First Published in Great Britain 2018
by Mills & Boon, an imprint of HarperCollins*Publishers*
1 London Bridge Street, London, SE1 9GF

© 2018 JC Harroway

ISBN: 978-0-263-93204-1

MIX
Paper from
responsible sources
FSC˙ C007454

This book is produced from independently certified FSC™ paper
to ensure responsible forest management.
For more information visit www.harpercollins.co.uk/green.

Printed and bound in Spain
by CPI, Barcelona

For D, who loved a good romance.

CHAPTER ONE

OLIVIA NOBLE WALKED behind the elderly professor, passing through the chrome-and-glass doors etched with the name of the swanky restaurant on the thirty-first floor of The Shard, London's tallest building. Her belly, jittery enough from the long, hair-raising elevator ride, flipped at the panoramic views dotted with the city's iconic landmarks. As a native New Yorker she accepted gravity-defying skyscrapers as part of life, but she avoided ones of this magnitude wherever possible.

'Ah, the others are still at the bar.'

Professor McBride gestured Libby ahead of him, towards the party of suits. Libby's legs wobbled on her four-inch heels as she crossed the plush carpet, trying to master the hold adrenaline had on her body. Her poor adrenal glands were wrung dry. This sophisticated, elegant restaurant might as well have been a roadside diner for all she noticed.

Head of her own marketing business in New York, she was used to public speaking. That didn't mean she enjoyed it, or that nerves hadn't gripped her for the whole forty-minute presentation she'd given this morn-

ing at the London Business School. In fact, she'd been
blown away when invited to speak at such a prestigious
seminar, unaware that anyone across the pond had even
heard of her small up-and-coming company.

The rest of the speakers were clustered at the bar, forming small huddles, deep in conversation. Several glanced
up as Libby and Professor McBride approached—faces
she recognised from the seminar, and one face in particular that demanded more than a fair share of her attention.
A face that was hard to ignore.

Alex Lancaster.

His stare lifted from the conversation taking place
before him, settling on her over the tops of the heads
separating them and practically stripping her bare. A
shiver originated in her ovaries and snaked south to
join the wobble in her legs. Those eyes... The intensity
with which they pierced the recipient of his undivided
attention...

Wow. Close up he was... *Wow*. A movie-star bad boy,
a gentleman rogue and a geeky surfer dude all rolled
into one mouthwatering package. Not that he had much
of the surfer dude on display at the moment, attired as
he was in a tailored three-piece suit that had probably
cost more than the annual mortgage payment on her
modest six-hundred-square-foot apartment. The only
nod to his wilder side was the slightly dishevelled flop
of dark hair, which looked as if it refused to be tamed,
no matter what he did.

Libby clenched her thighs together, her twitchy fingers gripping her bag.

'Glass of wine, my dear?' Professor McBride asked.

Libby nodded, her eyes hot as she stared back at Alex Lancaster for longer than was polite or wise. Likely she was not the only woman in the room who found that staring at this disarmingly attractive specimen of manhood pushed semipornographic visions into her head.

She rolled her shoulders and looked away, blinking the burn from her eyes. A snort gusted over her top lip. Who was she kidding? Her thoughts veered firmly towards the absolutely pornographic where he was concerned. She tugged at the hem of her tailored jacket. Time to get her head back in the game.

She was a professional, a well-respected member of the business community who owned her own successful marketing business—credentials that had prompted her invitation to London to speak at the 'Inspiring Business Leaders of the Future' seminar.

She darted her attention back to Professor McBride and his lengthy introductions to those closest, all the while willing her greedy eyes to stay away from the lure of Mr Lancaster, the only other person close to her age in the group.

Libby zoned out of the tedious conversation, discreetly blowing through pursed lips and lifting wisps of escaped hair from her too-warm face. How could that man have such a profound effect on her? Perhaps her PA was right, and she did need a 'good seeing to'. She'd have to give the perceptive Scotsman a raise, or finally sign up to that dating app he kept shoving in front of her.

Mmm...maybe not.

Fickle thoughts drifted back to the smokin' billionaire across the restaurant. Forget swiping left or right. She could just swipe him out of that suit, tangle her fingers in that too-long hair while she directed his smart, arrogant head south… The dark scruff covering his angular face scraping across her sensitive inner thighs…

Whew! Potent stuff. There must be something in the English water—it was the only explanation for her train of thought.

She cleared her perilously tight throat, yanking her mind out of the gutter, her gaze from the toes of her favourite shoes and her attention back to the drone of Professor McBride's voice.

'…and this is Alex Lancaster, one of our former golden boys, university benefactor and the major sponsor of today's seminar—although I'm sure he needs no introduction.'

Professor McBride's ass-kissing drawled to a close as his attention was requested by a university faculty member with a penchant for purple highlights and matching purple accessories.

Before she could mentally prepare herself for the close-up impact of his dazzling good looks, Alex had enclosed Libby's hand in his larger one, setting off a cascade of tingles; little flicks of flame dancing along her wrist and raising the hairs on her arm.

Damn…

Smokin' was an insult. Brains, business acumen and indecent levels of sex appeal—Alex Lancaster had certainly won the genetic lottery.

And of *course* she knew of him. *Everyone* knew of him. Besides, she'd done her research prior to flying in yesterday. One of Britain's youngest billionaires, he wasn't the richest, but his reputation for intuitive, if not somewhat reckless, business decisions was surpassed only by his brooding charisma and the dazzling smile that somehow managed to appeal to women of all ages.

Perhaps it was the single dimple in his cheek—simultaneously boyish and wicked. Or the incredible expressive eyes the colour of burnt sugar that regularly stared out from the glossy magazine covers he graced. Either way, he was utterly disarming. So much so that her voice completely deserted her—no doubt it was attending the 'Get Alex Lancaster Naked' rally being hosted by her libido and sponsored by her erogenous zones.

'Ms Noble. Great talk.'

His mouth kicked up, unleashing the full force of that dimple. Damn, that smile could melt the underwear clean off her body. And his voice: smoky…rich bourbon in a cut-glass tumbler.

Her sharp, tight-fitting suit—her signature outfit—transformed into a straitjacket. It was the only explanation for the hot flush misting her skin and the prickle of every tiny hair covering her body.

'Nice to meet you, Mr Lancaster.'

Libby pulled her hand from his. Not that the move offered relief from the inferno engulfing her. He was too close. Too virile. Too everything.

Get a grip, Libby. He's just another suit.

Right—if by 'suit' she meant a walking advertisement for 'Hot Boardroom Dudes'. Perhaps he could start an internet craze. She'd be the first to sign up.

'You deserve every scrap of your reputation.' He rubbed his knuckles over one lightly stubbled cheek, his dark gaze sparkling.

Libby's missing-in-action tongue returned to her mouth. 'Well, that's a rare talent, Mr Lancaster—one that the gossip rags and business pages fail to credit *you* with.'

Libby wiped her palm along the length of her skirt, her body half turned away from him so he wouldn't see the gesture that gave away the effect he had on her. The thought of this man's focus honed on her, even simply her online business profile, shunted heat to the most inconvenient places.

At his small frown, she continued. 'Perfectly disguising an insult within a compliment.'

She glanced over his shoulder, raising her eyebrows in acknowledgement of someone she recognised as she made to bypass him.

'Excuse me.'

Arrogant, sexy...

He laughed. A head-thrown-back bellow that forced more gold flecks into the burnt caramel of his irises.

A waiter blocked Libby's escape route with the delivery of her Pinot Gris, the elegant wine glass glistening with condensation. She bestowed her politest smile on the handsome waiter, still preparing to walk away from the charismatic jerk before her. Even if he *was* pleasing on the eye and the six-foot-three embodiment of most women's filthiest fantasises. Fantasies she'd never imagined until she'd slid her eyes over Mr Testosterone there.

'Forgive me…' His hand on her arm stilled her. 'What I should have said is that yours was by far the most entertaining of the lectures given this morning. I've heard of your work. I'm a businessman and I keep abreast of international business news.'

His mouth caressed the lip of his own wine glass, and he held her gaze over the rim, a mix of devilment and challenge warring for control in his slightly narrowed, sinfully provocative stare.

His hand, still on her arm, burned a hole through the fine wool of her favourite jacket. Large, tanned, with a sprinkling of dark hair smattering the wrist that poked from the cuff of his expensive linen shirt. Slight calluses marred the perfection of his long, elegant fingers, and she glimpsed clean square nails before he withdrew.

She had the absurd urge to ask him if he had a daily manicure. Was that how pampered British billionaires filled their days? Of course it was dwarfed by other urges that involved those large callused hands and her nipples.

It really had been too long…

Free from his touch, she regained her composure, her intellect wrestling it free from the clutches of her hormone-riddled body.

'I see. I'm sorry I can't return the compliment. I missed your talk.'

And she'd never worked for any IT giant. Why would she have crossed *his* radar?

Still looking at her as if his X-ray vision had burned holes through her clothing down to her lacy underwear, he shrugged one large shoulder.

His charcoal-grey suit encased his frame like a glove. She'd bet her beloved cat, Dumbledore, that it was cashmere—probably bespoke Savile Row. A copper-coloured tie brought out those ridiculous sparks of fire in his eyes and highlighted his decadent, cry-worthy black lashes.

Libby curled her fingers into her palms to stop herself fanning her flushed face.

Back to her escape plan.

As if anticipating her, he stepped sideways, facing her full-on, his broad chest eclipsing her vision. 'I'm glad I met you today. I'd like your professional advice, actually.'

He took another sip of wine, his bold stare raking her face and dipping to her throat. If he'd gone any lower this conversation would be over, regardless of his pretty face and intriguing request.

'Perhaps we could sit together...discuss it over lunch?' Then came the eyebrow lift. Perfectly executed, devastatingly tempting.

Had her body not reacted so overwhelmingly towards him, she might have agreed. The company he'd founded in his late teens, Lancaster IT, had gone global in recent years, with sales of its software to the Asian healthcare market shunting its drool-worthy founder and CEO from wealthy to obscene. Any business association her marketing company might have with the new IT giant making international waves would surely provide her with the kudos she needed to take her *own* business to the next level.

But she abhorred arrogance. Alex Lancaster was not

only renowned for fly-by-the-seat-of-his-pants business decisions that left wiser, more experienced competitors shaking in their hand-stitched Oxfords, but his personal life was equally reckless. Just thinking about this daredevil playboy's antics brought her out in an icy chill.

She demurred—after all, he *was* incredibly influential. 'I'm flattered. If you ask your assistant to call mine, I'm sure we can set something up.'

She took an embossed business card from her purse and passed it to him, careful to keep her fingertips away from the thrill of his.

'Although my personal client workload at present has me a little over-committed.'

What was she *saying*? This was a dream scenario for her small but growing business. Was she palming off an account of this magnitude on to one of her juniors? Seriously? All because he was twice as hot in person, made her thighs tremble and soaked her expensive lingerie—her one indulgence.

He flipped the card between his fingers in a continuous hypnotic loop of digital gymnastics. Mesmerising. What *else* could he do with those talented fingers?

Libby dragged her gaze away. His sexy stare was back. Pinning her heels to the carpet. Normally she tolerated awkward silences, especially in business settings. But he rocked her cool composure.

'It—It's all there…on my website.' *Babbling.* A successful twenty-eight-year-old businesswoman with a master's degree in marketing was babbling.

He didn't once glance at the card, which still tumbled lazily between his long, tanned fingers. 'I'd really like your personal input. You've done wonders for Kids Count.'

Why would her work for a small US charity interest him? Although it *had* landed her a prestigious industry award.

His lips caressed his wine glass, his eyes watching her over the rim. 'I'm involved with a charity too.'

He tucked the card into the inside pocket of his jacket, close to his chest.

The gesture, strangely intimate, made heat pool low in her belly. She definitely needed to get laid.

Tonight.

'I'm willing to pay.'

His talk of payment sealed the deal. 'I'm sorry.'

Heralding from one of the UK's most affluent families, and growing up in the family business, he had founded his first company on a ten thousand pound loan from his businessman father.

Well, some things weren't for sale.

No doubt he was used to getting everything he wanted. Calling the shots. Bossing people around. Well, not this chick.

Liar. He could boss her around in the bedroom any time.

'I'd be happy to connect you with Sonya, my top marketing executive and business partner—although she's soon to go on maternity leave so I suggest you get in quick.'

No way could she work personally with this man. Not after a simple glance across a room and a professional, perfectly polite handshake had triggered a full-blown hormone implosion. Images of them tangled in the crisp white sheets of her king-sized hotel bed rocked her back on her heels. Would he be as demanding in the bedroom? And would she concede, give him what he wanted? She could make a few sexual demands of her own...

The tip of his tongue traced along his lower lip—a snake-charming manoeuvre that held her gaze captive for long, silent seconds. She shook her head, dragging her eyes away.

Her libidinous thoughts stunned her. Perhaps he'd doused himself in genetically modified pheromones?

Time to get away from him and his unsettling magnetism.

'Nice to meet you.' Libby abandoned polite convention and kept her hand by her side. Best not to touch him again in case she needed to rush to the bathroom and put herself out of her own misery.

As if he knew her thoughts, he let a half grin dance on his twisted mouth. His chin lifted, lazy eyes raking her. 'The pleasure was all mine, Olivia.'

He delivered her name with a cut-crystal English accent and a side helping of gravel that spoke directly to all her wide-awake lady parts.

Libby winced, wishing her laptop's webcam would explode.

'You said *what*? Are you crazy?' Sonya rubbed her rounded belly, twisting on the sofa and putting her feet up on the low coffee table in Libby's New York office.

This video call and the five-hour time difference

between New York and London meant her right-hand woman was taking her lunch break, relaxing on Libby's sofa. Apparently it was more comfortable than the sofa in Sonya's office—although Libby suspected her friend just missed having her to bounce ideas off. They were a great team. More than that.

Sonya's face filled the screen as she leaned forward, peering through cyberspace. 'I can't possibly do that account justice in the time I have left.' She flopped back on the cushions, as if the act of merely speaking exhausted her. 'Why would you even suggest me? He clearly wants *you*. And you're there, on the ground.'

Sonya took a bite from her sandwich and shoved another cushion into the small of her back.

They usually ate lunch together on days when they were both in the office, discussing accounts and synching their diaries. Today, for some inexplicable reason— she blamed jet lag—Libby had shared the details of her meeting with Alex Lancaster and now had to pay the price.

'He's arrogant—and surprisingly rude for an Englishman.'

And sexy as fuck, with dreamy eyes, and an edge that made her want to defy him to see what happened…

'Throwing his money around.'

And looking at her as if she was a medium rare steak and he'd been living off beans for months.

Right, and she hadn't objectified *him* at all? His tight ass in his perfectly tailored trousers? No? Her gaze hadn't once dipped to the bulge at his crotch, wondering what lay beneath the fine fabric?

Of course she couldn't tell Sonya about her body's insane, treacherous reaction to him. Sonya had known Callum. She'd read something into her meeting with Alex Lancaster that simply hadn't been there. And she definitely couldn't confide her surprising fantasies to her bestie. She barely knew where they'd come from herself. No. It was just unfortunate timing.

Three years without sex really was too long. She hated to concede it, but her assistant, Vinnie, was right.

'So?' Her friend waggled a finger at the camera. 'It's business. This account and his contacts could help us expand into Europe, Asia—the world.'

Sonya's 'duh' look of incredulity soured Libby's tea—a less than satisfactory brew made from the meagre selection in her hotel room. She pushed it away, sipping water from a bottle instead, stalling for time.

Refusing to hear his proposal didn't make sense. *Business* sense. But instinct had brought her this far in her success story, and the same instinct told her to stay away from Alex Lancaster. He was just too charismatic, charming, virile. Nope. Her reaction to him this afternoon confirmed it; he was dangerous.

She didn't do danger. And despite his enormous accomplishments, she couldn't abide his reputation for recklessness.

'Well, if *you* take the account the effects for the company will be the same.' She plastered on her best convincing smile. 'There's a hefty bonus in it. Think of all the baby stuff you could buy.'

Wow, low blow, Libby. Cheap shot.

Sonya huffed. Probably she was too uncomfortable to appreciate the merits of Libby's inducements.

'No way. I won't have time. I'll end up handing it over to you anyway, when I go on maternity leave. And, to be honest, I should have quit by now. I don't want to have this baby in the elevator with only Vinnie for assistance. You know how he fusses. I'd end up killing him and *then* where would you be?'

A queasy roll of the stomach put an end to Libby's thoughts of popping out for dinner. She'd yet to find a temporary stand-in for Sonya—the would-be candidates they'd interviewed so far had been woefully inadequate to fill such capable shoes.

The pair were cut from the same cloth. Had studied at the same college. The same business school. When Libby had started out, Sonya had come on board and they'd created Noble and Pullman, investing in the joint venture, teaching each other as much as they'd learned from each other.

Any day now, there was going to be a substantial Sonya-shaped hole left in their small but precious company.

As if he'd heard his name mentioned, Vinnie, Libby's outspoken and at times frankly inappropriate PA, entered her office, poking his head over Sonya's shoulder so his face filled the screen. She waved, relieved to have a reprieve from justifying her inexplicable reluctance to work with Lancaster IT—or rather its sexy founder.

'How are things going, Vinnie? Any more responses?' She'd approached a few medium-sized firms here in London, hoping to drum up a little new business before she returned home in a few days.

'No' really.'

Vinnie spoke with a thick Scottish brogue she failed to understand most days.

'Do you want me to make some follow-up calls?'

Libby sighed. She was good at her job. Could sell anything. But still she sometimes struggled to sell herself. Never quite outgrowing her humble, wrong-side-of-the-tracks beginnings.

'No. I'll take care of it—and if I can't see anyone I'll just be a tourist for a few days. Perhaps I'll meet the Queen.'

She couldn't remember the last time she'd taken any holiday, and the two worried faces peering back at her from her laptop screen confirmed that her suggestion wasn't just alien to *her.*

She needed a change of subject, before Vinnie pulled up a list of London's singles clubs and Sonya told her—again—that it was 'time to move on'.

'Are you taking care of Sonya?'

Her friend's eyes rolled.

Vinnie smiled. 'Well, you know what she's like... Let's just say I'm trying. If I end up delivering this wee one...' he stroked Sonya's belly and she batted him away '...I want a bonus.'

They all chuckled, but the sound held a nervous undertone. Libby shouldn't have left the helm at such a crucial time. She'd been lured by the all-expenses-paid trip to a city she'd always dreamed of visiting and had been flattered that they'd asked for her personally to speak at the conference.

'I came in to tell you I've had Alex Lancaster on the phone this morning. He called asking for your personal number,' said Vinnie.

Libby straightened in her chair, her heart thumping double time.

'Don't worry, hen. I didn't give it to him—although he's a determined young fella.'

Libby pressed her lips together. Vinnie needed no encouragement for the ridiculous things he said. 'Young fella' hardly did Alex Lancaster justice.

'He seemed to know where you're staying, so he may call. Said he had a "business proposition".' Vinnie made air quotes, a small smirk on his face. 'And wanted to discuss it before you left the UK.'

The one mouthful of tepid tea she'd managed sloshed inside Libby's hollow insides.

Sonya's eyes rounded to the size of her pregnant belly. She lumbered into a sitting position, glaring into the webcam. 'He *really* wants you.' Her shrewd eyes narrowed.

Libby chewed her lip, evading comment. The last thing she needed was this unlikely pair of would-be matchmakers getting the wrong idea about Alex Lancaster's intentions and her own position. She'd already said too much.

Flutters invaded her chest at the thought of speaking to him, of seeing him again. *Stop.* She didn't have to take his call. She'd already heard his proposition. Her answer would be the same.

With that, the hotel phone rang on the desk next to her, making all three of them jump. She stared at the device for two or three rings, frozen. It had to be him. No one else knew where she was, with the exception of the two people staring at her with excitement and intrigue shining in their eyes.

'Answer it,' Sonya said, gesturing wildly at Libby to accept the call.

They waited. Expectant. Sometimes it sucked that these two knew her so well.

Rolling her shoulders back, she chided herself. Act professional. He was just a businessman. Just another potential client. Libby covered her mouth with her index finger, shushing them. Then turned the laptop away so it faced the wall. Sonya and Vinnie would hear her side of the conversation, but they wouldn't see her face while she answered the call.

'Libby Noble.' *Shit*, her voice was all breathy—as if she'd run a marathon.

She relaxed her clenched fingers, slipping her feet from her shoes under the desk and flexing her toes into the plush pile of the carpet. Libby's neck burned, just knowing that Sonya and Vinnie were listening from the laptop beside her. They'd worked and played alongside her for the last four years, seeing her at her best and at her worst. Although the 'play' had been virtually non-existent since Callum's death.

'Olivia—Alex Lancaster here.'

His voice rasped down the line, scraping at her earlobe. She rolled her eyes. Why couldn't he have a normal voice? A boring monotone that left her cold?

Libby cleared her tight throat. 'Mr Lancaster.' That was better. Clipped, curt, taking no shit. 'How can I help you?'

He chuckled. The bastard actually *chuckled*. 'You *can* call me Alex, you know.'

His voice was huskier over the phone, his dashing accent stronger—or perhaps without the visual distraction, her senses were more acutely attuned to every nuance of him.

Fantastic.

'I hoped to persuade you to reconsider my offer.'

Just listening to him speak made her think of sex. His voice, deep and authoritative, screamed control. It should be a real turn-off. She hated being told what to do. Perhaps it was the change in time zones, messing with her biorhythms. She smoothed a crease from her skirt, her restless fingers needing something to do. Something other than itching to twist through his decadent flop of hair.

'I thought we'd concluded things this morning.'

'Had we?'

All she'd really concluded was that she was ridiculously attracted to him, and that her hormones were securely at the helm, sailing the Libby ship into uncharted waters. Waters fraught with wild fantasies. Just a hint of danger. Enough to thrill.

'I wanted to tell you a bit more about the project. I think I mentioned I'm chief executive of a charity based here in London.'

Had he? She'd been too focussed on the rasp of his hand and the head-rush caused by his spicy scent.

'It's called Able-Active. Have you heard of it?'

Libby spun a pen on the desk, its hypnotic circling matching the frequency and rhythm of Alex's rumbling speech. Autocratic, imposing, seductive... She could listen to him for hours...especially if he talked dirty.

'No, I'm sorry. I haven't.'

Her own voice was relatively low and husky for a woman. But his curled itself around her like a comfort blanket—warm, sensual and with just enough scrape to bring to life every nerve ending in her body. Particularly those tightly clustered between her legs.

'Yes. And there's my problem. At the moment the charity can only accept participants from the South East. I want to extend it throughout the UK's other major cities. There are a lot of kids with different needs out there, Olivia—kids who deserve the experiences Able-Active provides.'

He'd pricked her interest. 'What kind of charity?'

She quickly typed Able-Active into the search engine on her mobile phone and brought up the website.

'It's for kids with all kinds of different abilities. A recreational adventure centre, outward bound type of thing.'

'I see. Well, I wish you luck with that venture, Mr Lancaster. It sounds very worthwhile.'

Damn him—couldn't he have a few obvious flaws? Bad breath, poor taste, a warped sense of humour...?

'It *is* worthwhile and...'

He paused, as if he sought the right word. Perhaps Mr Ruthless McReckless had a soft centre...

'It's important to me. That's why I want the best people working on it.'

Ooh, flattery.

'I've done my research. The best people is *you*. I read about your award. And the CEO of Kids Count wrote a very flattering piece about you in *Charity Times*.'

Silence settled, thick and cloying, pushing Libby back into the chair. Of *course* he'd researched her. He'd hinted as much this morning with his comment about her reputation. He was an astute businessman, intuitive, quick witted, driven. Any self-respecting would-be employer would do his homework.

She'd done the same; spent most of the afternoon scouring the internet and his website. Of course she'd missed any mention of his charity work. Too busy drooling over pictures of him shirtless on some exotic island. Too focussed on replaying his TED talks over and over just to hear the scrape of his voice. And too absorbed in imagining what he looked like under his urbane business suits.

This smacked of a personal crusade. No. He probably applied the same drive and determination to any enterprise he was involved with.

She remained silent. Why this reluctance to work with him? He brought something out in her—some perverse streak of her personality that revelled in denying his wishes. A battle of wills? Not very mature of her and bad for business.

'Any number of firms could handle that kind of strategy.'

Yes, she'd worked on a campaign for the American

charity, but surely he could find what he needed here in the UK.

He gave a small sigh. 'Look, I get what I want, Olivia. You've proved yourself to have a clear and savvy understanding of the current social media climate. You have a flair for clever and innovative imagery and Kids Count are benefitting markedly. I want the same for my charity.'

His charity?

'That's why I put your name forward to the London Business School when they approached me to speak at today's seminar.'

She stifled a gasp. *He'd* personally recommended her? And, as he sponsored the conference, *he'd* flown her here all expenses paid—including this hotel room. Her gaze skittered to the bed. The image of him naked and sprawled there, telling her what he wanted with that upper crust voice of his made her heart hammer. Not that she'd give it to him.

I get what I want. His arrogance…

Again, her mind veered. *Did* he want her? Fantasise about them together as she'd done since the moment she'd met him? Well, as much as it would cost her, both professionally and personally, she'd have to show him he didn't always get what he wanted.

She cleared her throat. 'Well, I hope you have yourself the best accountant over there at Able-Active. Not many start-up charities have such a large marketing budget.'

Her personal services didn't come cheap, no matter how attractive the man paying the check.

'You let me worry about that. Can you start tomorrow?'
Arrogant, presumptive asshole.

'Mr Lancaster. Throwing money at me won't change my mind.'

If anything, it made her inclined to hang up. Unlike Mr Sexy Billionaire, *she* hadn't lived a privileged childhood full of skiing holidays and the right private schools. Her daddy didn't own a super-yacht—in fact, she didn't *have* a daddy. Like her single parent mother, she'd worked hard every day for everything she had, and she appreciated every cent she spent—despite the designer clothes she wore and her top-of-the-range car. *Frivolous* was not a word in Libby's vocabulary.

'Well, what *will* change your mind?'

His voice dropped to a sultry drawl. The one she imagined was his bedroom voice.

Imagined or hoped?

Had he asked her to work for his IT company she'd have already ended this conversation. Her eyes drifted over the images on the Able-Active website. Smiling faces…kids joyously experiencing the thrill and accomplishment of some outdoor adventure.

'It's very important to me, Olivia.'

The way he spoke her name—her full name—as if it was their little secret.

'Why?' She whispered the request, as if the intimacy of his answer warranted such secrecy. Alex Lancaster—full of intriguing contradictions?

'Personal reasons.' The pitch of his voice lifted a fraction. 'I had a sister.'

Had?

'Let me offer a sweetener.'

He didn't want to talk about his sister. This she understood. She had no-go areas in her past too.

'Lancaster IT's marketing contract is up for renewal in two months. If you help me out with Able-Active the contract is yours.'

She gasped. 'Regardless of how good my work is? That's ridiculous.'

Was he mad? How had he become so successful so young? Rash decisions and financial extravagance wouldn't have cut it. She'd been right about him. Reckless.

'Just do what you did for Kids Count and I'll be happy.'

Mmm... What would a happy Alex look like? Libby vacillated. Sonya was right. A high-profile account like his would shunt their company into the big league. Finally reward them for years of hard work. Surely she could control her startling attraction to him for long enough to get the job done and get out? And hadn't she been hoping to attract new business while here in the UK? This was a dream scenario landing in her lap.

Still she wavered.

A compromise?

'Perhaps Sonya could mock up some drafts and I'll step in once she goes on maternity leave.'

That made no sense. What was *wrong* with her? She flushed, knowing Sonya could hear the gibberish coming out of her mouth. Libby was here. Sonya was in New York and about to deliver her baby any day.

'I want *you*.'

Not fair.

She closed her eyes as her overactive libido spun off into fantasyland, taking her pounding heart along for the ride. How would it feel to be the recipient of that bare statement in another time, another context? Would he give her what her body clearly craved? A couple of mind-blowing orgasms? Nothing more. Would she concede to his control, loosen the tight command she subjected every aspect of her own life to just for one blissful minute? Give him everything?

She slowed her rapid breaths and mentally slapped herself. She was a hard-assed career woman. She employed twenty people, won lucrative contracts and industry awards. She didn't crumble when faced with an attractive employer. No matter how intense his golden eyes or how sin-dipped his gravelly voice. And, these days, she never conceded control. It wasn't worth the risk.

But this made good business sense. A connection of this visibility would allow her to pick and choose Sonya's stand-in. And by the time her friend returned from maternity leave they'd be ready to take on the world.

She'd have to be careful. Despite her daydreams, a man like Alex would quickly take anything she gave.

She sucked in a breath, confident in her abilities to handle him. Decided, she was all business.

'I'll have my assistant contact yours to make the arrangements.' Libby lifted her chin, although she knew he couldn't see the gesture.

'I'll have the contracts drawn up.'

She could almost hear his victory grin slither down the phone line.

'Pleasure doing business with you, Mr Lancaster.'

She hung up, all the air leaving her in rush, one word lingering in her dry mouth. *Pleasure*. Would it be?

When her face felt cooler to the touch, she turned back to her laptop screen and her colleagues.

Their grins said it all.

Damn. What had she done?

CHAPTER TWO

ALEX LANCASTER STOPPED the treadmill and reached for the towel he'd thrown over the handrail, using it to the wipe the sting of sweat from his eyes. He preferred to run in the Oxfordshire countryside, or along the banks of the River Thames. But on the nights when he stayed in the city his office treadmill just had to suffice. And today he needed to push himself twice as hard to out-run the restlessness.

Despite his forty-minute workout, thoughts of the enigma that was Olivia Noble had dogged his every step.

Briefly checking his phone for urgent messages, he clicked off the TV that dominated one wall of his spacious office, silencing the business news, and headed for the en-suite shower.

Alex ducked his head under the pounding spray, ignoring the flicker of interest from his cock—a renewed flicker brought on by the curvy, sophisticated brunette. He'd admired her enough from afar, but in person she'd blown him away. Sassy, shrewd, cutting through his bullshit, as she'd no doubt call it.

He closed his eyes, recalling the sexy timbre of her husky voice. She spoke as if she had a bad case of laryngitis or a lifelong smoking habit. She didn't have either. He'd scoured every detail he could find about her on the internet, filling in the blanks with his vivid, slightly perverted imagination.

An imagination inspired by the thick, glossy dark hair she wore fastened at her nape in an elegant ponytail, by the provocative curve of her rounded hips concealed by the figure-hugging pencil skirts she wore and the tiny glimpse of pale, creamy cleavage he'd seen that morning when she'd moved away from him, her blouse tugging across her breasts and revealing just enough to make him hard for the rest of the day.

Of course their verbal spat on the phone hadn't helped either.

He scrubbed shampoo into his scalp, his fingertips punishing. He'd never had to work so hard to entice someone to work with him. His employees loved him. He gave them stellar health insurance cover, more holidays than were legally required and fat bonuses for a job well done. He even offered his top software designers and their families a week's stay a year at his boutique winery in Oxfordshire as a loyalty inducement. Consequently, he retained his best staff in what was a highly competitive global industry.

Olivia Noble had almost sounded *insulted* when he'd discussed her fee. Surely she wasn't that naive? Like it or not, money made the world go round—any good businessperson knew that. And, from his research,

Olivia certainly deserved the title—something that doubled her allure in his mind.

She had graduated first in her year with a Bachelor of Commerce degree, had a master's degree in marketing, and in four years had taken her company from a start-up to one of the top ten marketing firms in New York. Her work on the high-profile Kids Count charity had dragged her from obscurity to his attention.

Did her reluctance have anything to do with the sparks of chemistry that seemed to arc between them? Did she feel it too? That almost frenzied pull?

He soaped himself more vigorously, turning the dial on the shower down to tepid, to cool the blaze she'd evoked.

She'd wanted nothing to do with him earlier today. He'd planned to woo her to work with him over the lunch put on by the Business School. But she'd acted as if she couldn't get away quickly enough. Straight talking, no simpering or inane flattery.

And hadn't that been a big fucking turn-on? Another point in Ms Noble's favour.

Most women he met struggled to conceal the spark of excitement in their eyes, as if in meeting him they'd been handed a winning lottery ticket. Sadly, regardless of how attractive they were or how much they shared in common, he could never quite be sure their interest was in him the person or him the young entrepreneur listed on *Forbes*.

Not that Olivia had been able to fully conceal the flush of her chest or the rapid flutter of the pulse in her neck. He'd felt it too. The immediate slug of fascination that had had his head swivelling in a double-take the minute she'd stepped onto the stage to deliver her speech to the packed auditorium of keen undergraduates.

And close up… He'd had to discreetly adjust his cock in his slim-fit trousers as she'd walked away from their frustratingly brief interaction, trailing a light floral scent in her wake. He'd wanted to follow her, his nose to the ground like a bloodhound, sniffing at her sexy four-inch stilettos.

Roughly towelling himself dry, he analysed their arduous phone conversation. *Why* was the delectable Ms Noble so reluctant to take the account? He'd seen her body of work. She was amply capable of running both the Able-Active marketing strategy *and* that of Lancaster IT. The majority of her current client base was situated in the States. Surely she saw the benefits of expanding globally? And why had her initial refusal stung his modest ego? Lancaster IT ranked in the *Financial Times* 'Global 500', so it couldn't be his professional credentials.

He slipped into jeans and a clean shirt, selecting a blazer from the supply he kept at work. He grabbed his phone, frustration mounting. He'd grown accustomed to getting what he wanted, and if things went against him, he made them work. Refused to give up.

Perhaps Olivia's aversion was to him personally.

No, that didn't make sense. She hadn't been able to hide her body's unconscious reaction any more than he'd been able to hide his. She *must* share his personal interest—

her reluctance was for mixing the two. But they were similar in many ways. Driven. Career-focussed.

He'd just have to convince her they could have the best of both worlds. That they needed to scratch this itch and then put it aside and focus on the important work ahead. Rewarding work. Work that would make a real difference and allow him to put some of his wealth into creating change. Or at least help him atone for Jenny...

He swallowed, forcing his mind away from a well-worn, unwanted path. He had to move forward. Use past mistakes to make good future decisions.

He blew out a slow, controlled sigh, his mind returning to Olivia. She'd eventually relented, her manner turning brisk, putting him in his place.

His cock twitched again, and impatience urged him to fire a brief text to his driver.

By the time he was seated in the back of his car, speeding through the streets of London, now devoid of rush-hour traffic, he'd formulated a charm offensive.

If a lucrative business deal couldn't tempt out her reluctant smile, he'd have to find other inducements.

Libby sighed. Her fingers absently swirled the stirrer in her martini and the general hubbub of the hotel bar behind her faded to background noise.

She'd longed to sleep, to enjoy the luxurious tub in her deluxe room and put today behind her. But, jet-lagged, fractious and horny from her encounters with Alex, sleep had drifted further out of reach with each passing minute. The alcohol wouldn't help—not with the sleeplessness *or* the horniness—but sitting in the impersonal confines of her beige room, thinking about Alex and his offer, wasn't an option.

It was a good offer. Before meeting him she'd have jumped at it. But now...?

The more time she spent with the captivating businessman, the greater the risk of her succumbing to her attraction to him. An attraction as alarming as it was alluring. Alex Lancaster wasn't the type of man to take no for an answer, and her yes wasn't given lightly these days.

Someone invaded her personal space.

'Why don't you drink that so I can buy you another one?' the man in the suit said, leaning too close and wafting her with beer-fume breath.

Great, this was the last thing she needed. She looked up, unsmiling. Why did guys assume a woman alone in bar must clearly be waiting for them? He was cute enough, if you ignored the leer and the breath, but her body couldn't muster one drop of enthusiasm for the predictable stranger.

The same body that had spent the entire day lusting after Alex Lancaster. The same body that still reminded her with soaked panties and chafed nipples that it had been three long years since she'd sought pleasure with another. Perhaps that was the reason Alex had got to her with little more than a raised eyebrow or the twist of his kissable lips.

Impervious to her go-away stare, Beer Breath slid one hand to the centre of her back and leaned over to reach for her phone, which was on the bar beside her untouched martini. Her hand beat his there. *Just*.

He pouted, swaying closer to bump shoulders with her. 'I was only going to give you my number, so you can call me when you've finished stirring that one to death and I can buy you another.'

He raised bushy eyebrows, the leer widening.

'Right…' Libby shrugged, shaking his hand from between her shoulder blades. 'But I'm fine.'

He grinned, signalling the barman.

Damn. He wasn't going to give up without a fight. That bath and the beige walls of her room looked increasingly appealing now. She should at least try to sleep. She'd need all her wits tomorrow—dealing with Alex would sap every scrap of resolve she possessed.

'I'm so sorry I'm late.'

The man occupying her thoughts swept up beside her on a cloud of freshly showered deliciousness, his hand taking a proprietorial hold of the back of her barstool and his smoky, heavy-lidded smile stripping her naked.

Alex.

'Hi.' Libby closed her slack-jawed mouth and swivelled to face him, turning her back on the stranger, never one to pass up a golden opportunity. She hated rudeness, but if Beer Breath was too stubborn or thick-skulled to take the hint…

Alex kept his stare on her, his smile genuine and warm enough to melt her underwear clean off, and then signalled the waiter with a flick of his wrist.

Libby sensed the moment when Beer Breath slinked away, and the hairs on the back of her neck settled—but only temporarily, because Alex hadn't taken his eyes off her. In fact, he was looking at her as if he was seconds from devouring her whole.

She shivered, delicious tendrils snaking to all her erogenous zones. 'What are you doing here?' Libby took a slug of her previously untouched drink, the burn calming her enough to meet his bold stare with one of her own.

'I came to invite you out for a late supper. I was on my way to Reception and then I spotted you here.' His hand slid from the back of her stool, and he settled into the one next to her, passing his order to the waiter before returning his disconcerting focus to her.

She stared back, lost for words and missing the proximity of his hand on her chair. He was close enough that his warmth traversed the space between them, but far enough away that she battled her body's urge to sway closer. And keep on swaying.

'What?' One corner of his mouth kicked up. 'What kind of host would I be if I left you to fend for yourself on your first night in a strange city?'

She couldn't help the snort that left her. 'The non-stalker kind…?'

He took the jibe with a cocksure arch of one brow, sipping wine while his poised stare flicked over her face from feature to feature.

Libby flushed hot all over. The 'stalker' comment had been beneath her. He hadn't once touched her, hadn't bought her drink, hadn't tried to grab her phone, hadn't even chased away her unwanted admirer—he had simply given her the out she'd wanted. The rest was all *her*.

What was *wrong* with her? Rudeness to a generous host and influential employer? All because he'd awoken needs within her? Needs too long dormant. Needs she'd never had before. Needs threatening to overwhelm her in their intensity.

Hardly his fault.

He dropped the bland smile, and a small frown crinkled the skin between his brows. 'It's a public bar, Olivia. I'm being a gentleman. But if you don't want company, just say so and I'll leave.'

He shrugged.

Simple.

Of course he would. Alex Lancaster didn't need to stalk women. They probably lined up, forming a polite, orderly, English queue.

She swallowed, her throat tight. 'Thank you.' She tilted her head in the direction of Beer Breath's exit path. 'He was about to become a persistent pain in my ass.'

He barely acknowledged the man in the suit, and his continued casual perusal made her limbs jittery and lodged a ball of restless energy low in her belly.

'So, have you eaten? Dinner?' One eyebrow lifted and he licked red wine from his plush lower lip.

A simple invitation. One she'd offer herself to a visiting business colleague new in town. Why, then, did it feel like more than an offer of a shared meal? Or was that simply her overactive libido filling in the blanks?

'I'm not hungry.' Her voice emerged as barely a croak.

No argument, no persuasion.

'Tell me…' He leaned a little closer, his stare a little

more penetrating, searching hers. 'Why the reluctance to work for Able-Active?'

Alex cut straight to the heart of an issue. She admired that. But no way could she explain her reticence without giving away a whole heap of personal stuff. Stuff she did her best never to think about.

She ducked her head away from his intensity, her sleeveless, lightweight blouse as cloying as a thick, woolly sweater.

He ploughed on. 'You think I'm arrogant.'

A statement. ·

She shot him a glance, surprised to see amusement lingering on his face.

He gave another shrug, as if he had her all worked out. 'I see it in your eyes.' He rested his elbows on the bar, leaning closer. 'I'd like you to extend your stay. All expenses covered, of course.'

'Why?' Her head spun, reeling from the arrogant request.

Hadn't they already established that she wouldn't roll over and do whatever he asked? If he didn't seem to have a hotline to her long-dormant libido she'd laugh in his sinfully handsome face.

'Able-Active doesn't happen inside an office. I want you to experience it, to really understand my vision. I'd like you to stay a fortnight.'

He took another sip of wine, giving her time to respond.

Her jaw fell, her fidgety hand stilling around the stem of her martini glass. 'Are you *nuts*?'

Clearly Libby was nuts, too, because for a fleeting

moment she considered it. Then she sobered. Even if
she wanted to jump when he clicked his fingers, she
couldn't. She had Sonya, her heavily pregnant partner,
to consider. Yes, she could work from anywhere in the
world with a Wi-Fi connection for short periods and,
yes, she'd cleared her desk before flying to the UK, but
a fortnight away from the office…

He laughed—a deep rumble that curled her toes and
transformed him from sexy, assured businessman to
sexy boy-next-door, all grown up. He turned his stool
to face her, leaning back in a relaxed slouch, his thighs
spread.

In invitation?

Libby's eyes burned with the effort of maintaining
eye contact and not succumbing to a visual tour of his
denim-clad crotch. Time to be clear. If this working
relationship was to be successful, he needed to understand a few things.

'You know, I'm sure you're used to it, but you can't
always have your own way.'

She plucked the olive from her drink, holding it between her teeth while she stared him down. Two could
play Mr Lancaster's game. If he thought she'd simper
at his flattery, drop to her knees no questions asked, he
wasn't as smart as she knew him to be.

She bit into the salty olive, allowing her tongue to
linger on her lips.

His pupils dilated—a subconscious tell over which
he had no control. Then he shrugged, as if he didn't
care either way. But she knew that wasn't true. Like
her, he'd likely achieved his success by expanding con-

trol over all areas of his life. Personal and professional. But did he *need* that control, like her? Did he feel as if he was spinning off into the inky blackness of space without it, like her?

He tilted his head, his astute gaze leaving her mouth at last. This time when he met her eyes she wanted to curl up and hide.

'I'll make you a proposition.' He lifted the glass to his lips, taking a sip while his words sank in.

Libby shook her head, determined to wrestle back the upper hand. 'I've conceded enough to you in our short acquaintance.'

Alex bit his lip, hiding a smile.

Bastard.

He flared his nostrils, sucking in a breath and tilting his head back to consider the ceiling. *Good.* She posed a challenge—no doubt a novelty to someone in his position. She could almost hear the cogs working in his head.

'Fair point.' He rubbed his index and middle finger along his lower lip. 'How about for every concession you make, I'll make one too?'

He shifted, his thighs parting a fraction more, as if he were growing uncomfortable. Was she having a similar effect on him as he had on her?

His voice dropped. Slow. Deep. Intimate.

'Equal. Mutually satisfying.'

He took another sip of wine. Waiting. Watching her over the rim.

Libby recrossed her legs, her thighs clammy. 'A negotiation? I warn you, I'm good.'

Not that she had any experience with *this* kind of deal. How to be a high school sweetheart, how to be a girlfriend, how to be a fiancée—yes. But how to handle this searing sexual chemistry and keep enough distance to emerge unscathed? Could he tell she was making this up as she went along?

He grinned.

Thought he had this in the bag, did he?

He gave a slow nod. 'I know that. Research, remember? The best.' He leaned forward, closing the distance between them, his voice a low whisper, eyes aglow. 'What do you say? Up for a little…adventure?'

Her mind raced, her heart beating its way into her throat.

Yes.

No.

'It depends…'

Were they even still talking about work? Did it matter? Perhaps Sonya, Vinnie and her hormones were right. A no-strings dalliance was exactly what she needed—slake this intense thirst she'd thought long extinguished, then finish a rewarding and lucrative job and move on.

As if he'd read her mind, he said, 'Come on.'

Libby leaned closer. His low voice called to her, zinging straight between her legs. From this distance, she could see his pulse flicking in the notch at the base of his throat, the dark hairs peeking over the open neck of his shirt, could smell the detergent he used on his laundry.

His voice continued—persuasive, tempting. 'You're a perceptive, intelligent woman...'

She braced one foot on the floor, her body swaying towards his as if she was hard of hearing and needed to lean closer to his tantalising mouth. Her hand landed on his thigh, steadying her balance, but the denim was a poor barrier to the heat and bulk of his taut muscles.

'You feel this insane chemistry too.' His stare smouldered, his breath tickling her neck.

She practically sagged into him. She wasn't alone. Wasn't imagining this. But should she act on it? Did she dare?

'I want you.' He held eye contact, his stark statement hanging in the crackling air between them. 'Physically, professionally.'

He spoke as if he was negotiating a business deal. Calm, collected, poker-faced.

A tiny shrug of one shoulder. 'Stay.'

He made it sound so easy—a foregone conclusion. And she was sorely tempted.

All the time they'd talked, he hadn't touched her. His hands were still relaxed on the arms of the barstool when all she wanted to do was slide her fingers through his silky dishevelled hair and angle his head until he kissed her. Kissed away the doubt. Kissed away the memories. Kissed away the loneliness.

She sat back, her hand slipping from the rock-hard muscles of his thigh. Time to wrestle this back under her command. Get a grip of herself and this situation. Give him a taste of his own medicine.

The trouble was, lust had robbed her brain of its usual

quick wit and all the negotiating skills she'd bragged about. Every single comeback or demand had fled her mind like sand falling through the holes of a sieve.

Perhaps she'd transmitted her thoughts telepathically to him, because he said, 'You need control?'

Could he see her that clearly? Were her fears, her hang-ups, so clearly displayed on her face?

He'd dropped the smile, his expression now serious, as if he understood the momentous battle raging inside her. She wanted him too—had spent the day thinking about him, about what it would be like to feel his touch, feel his mouth, feel him move inside her...

The urge to give in to that curiosity, that need, was overwhelming.

He dipped his chin, ensuring that she saw him—saw both the sincerity in his stare and the flare of the same battle inside him.

'I'm man enough to concede it. What can I do to give you what you need so we can both win?'

A silent groan had Libby's eyes drooping as she took in a long, ragged breath. What an intoxicating offer. Could she *do* this? Separate business from pleasure? Keep things casual between them? On *her* terms? Give him a concession or two and take what he was willing to concede?

She opened her eyes to his continued stare. The slight flare of his nostrils was the only sign that he too experienced the anticipation that fluttered in Libby's belly, bringing her to life.

Until she spoke, she was clueless as to how she'd respond. 'I'll give you a week.'

A week?

He nodded. So accommodating. So skilled at negotiating this fragile truce.

But she, too, could strike a pretty deal. Time to see
how much he was willing to relinquish. Could he be
a man of his word? Was he really interested in a deal?
Did he want her enough to agree to her terms?

There was only one way to find out.

She leaned closer, her lips parting on a barely there
gasp as their knees made contact. She dropped her voice,
as he'd done. 'If we're working together...' her eyes
flicked to his crotch, still displayed before her '...and
fucking, I won't be bossed around.'

Another nod. Another delicious concession.

Her mind raced, searching for a compromise that,
as he'd put it, would allow them both to get what
they wanted. She'd never fought so hard. Her self-
preservation demanded every inch of ground acquired.

The ultimate test of his mettle would come. Could
he withstand what she had planned for him? Would
her nerve hold?

Libby's temperature reached boiling point, seconds
away from spontaneous combustion. She shook her head
slowly, commanding his full attention. 'You won't get
your own way all the time.'

He shrugged again, the small half-smile returning.
'If I had my way...' he lifted his wine glass, taking a
sip, his eyes slowly raking over her mouth '...I'd have
fucked you at the top of The Shard this morning. Had
you screaming my name with that sexy voice of yours.'

Her gasp sounded so loud she expected the whole population of the bar to turn in their direction.

He quirked a scornful brow. 'Seems to me, *you* are the one getting her way, Olivia.'

Danger. He reeked of it. Not that her personal safety was in question. But she should run all the same.

Still he stared, his eyes flicking between hers. Still her breaths gusted in and out through parted lips. She held his searing eye contact. A challenge. Battle lines being drawn.

Finishing her martini in one swallow, she slid from the stool, coming to stand between his still spread thighs. She leaned close, her heavy ponytail falling forward, a few strands of hair getting caught in the stubble covering his strong jaw.

With her lips mere millimetres from his ear, she whispered, a thrill tingling up her spine.

'*Quid....*'

Closer.

'*Pro...*'

She could almost feel the fine hairs on his earlobe tickle her lips.

'*Quo...*'

Leaning back, she took the key card from her purse and pressed it into his palm, turned on her heel and left the bar on shaky legs.

CHAPTER THREE

HE'D NEVER KNOW how he managed the walk from the bar and across the hotel foyer with his steely hard-on, but he caught up with Libby in two strides. He deliberately didn't touch her. Hadn't touched her all evening, although it had almost killed him. But she'd touched him.

Her handprint still burned his thigh, scorched clean though the denim and spoke directly to his cock. The brush of her bare knees, the scent wafting up from her thick, luxuriant hair… He groaned, digging into deep reserves for discipline over his body.

She walked close. Her arm brushed his and the sway of that long, lustrous ponytail tapped his shoulder in time with the clack of her heels across the marble tiles.

They reached the lifts. He pressed the call button, dragging her light floral scent into his lungs until the head rush made him close his eyes for a split second. *Fuck.* He needed to pull himself together, to grapple back some semblance of mastery. At least over his libido.

He mimicked her, staring straight ahead, his eyes

trained on the digital display as the numbers fell, heralding the lift's arrival.

His mouth burned to kiss her. To see if her plump, pouty lips tasted as good as they'd looked when she whispered the word *fucking*. On the surface she oozed cool, untouchable sophistication. Not a glorious hair out of place or a wrinkle in sight. But the deal she'd brokered— bold, assertive, knowing what she wanted—what a turn-on. Perhaps it was an American thing. Perhaps it was pure Olivia.

Quid pro quo.

That should have raised his hackles, but he was keen to discover her brand of give and take.

Perhaps he was losing his mind. But, oh, how he'd love to mess her up—to tug out that hair tie and slide his hands through those long, silky tresses, to feel them slither over his face, his chest, his abdomen while she kissed him... How would that austere exterior crack at the height of passion? With her full lips swollen by his kisses, her luminous eyes glazed and punch-drunk? Her smoky voice calling his name with that native New York accent of hers?

At this rate, he'd need a cold shower just to remain in her company. What did she have planned for him? Would he be able to keep it together?

The lift arrived. As the doors opened he saw the car was empty. He cast a glance sideways. He waited, hand out, inviting her to step inside first, all the while battling the urge to push her up against the wall and fuck her right there in the elegant foyer of the Windsor Hotel, Park Lane.

You won't get your own way all the time.

Right now, he'd gladly take ten per cent. Used to controlling every aspect of his life, especially his sex life, he knew this game he'd agreed to would test every ounce of his willpower.

As if she knew the direction of his thoughts, she poked her tongue out, sliding it along her lower lip, flooding his groin with fresh heat. She stepped inside and he followed, his hands forming fists by his sides to stop himself from touching her.

Doomed. He was *so* doomed.

If she looked down she'd see the effect this negotiation had had on him. The effect *she* had on him. He longed to readjust himself in his jeans, but he couldn't break the spell she'd wound around him as surely as if he was already tangled up in a cloud of that glorious hair. What would she look like naked? With that silky, decadent ponytail liberated until it covered her bare shoulders, the tips brushing her breasts?

She stepped in front of him, leaning over to press the button for her floor. The arch of her long, graceful neck called to him. The phantom taste of her skin lingered on his lips as if he'd already indulged.

He sucked in a breath through flared nostrils, turning to stare at her. *Fuck*, she was irresistible. Sassy, smart, sexy as hell and completely unimpressed by him. Most women he dated suffocated him with their cloying need to please. To be exactly what they thought he wanted. Olivia Noble didn't care *what* he wanted, and good for her. She called the shots. She spoke plainly. He'd never met a woman like her.

She stared back with a momentary flash of hesi-
tancy and a series of blinks of those long lashes over
rounded eyes. His chest pinched at this tiny hint of her
vulnerability. But he wouldn't let her off the hook. She'd
started this, raised the stakes. And he'd agreed to play
give and take—not his usual style—instinct telling him
she needed to stay in control at all times.

Why? He'd have to flex his patience if he wanted the
answer to that secret.

His body strained, every muscle primed to close the
deal. To put them both out of their misery and taste her.
But he knew the prize on her terms would be worth the
wait, the sacrifice.

She heard his prayer.

Stepping up to him, her bottom lip trapped beneath
her teeth, she slowly tunnelled her fingers into his hair.
The bite of pain tingled over his scalp as she twisted
the strands and angled his head. Her dark stare be-
witched him. She reached up on tiptoes and slid her
mouth over his, eyes open. Bold, demanding—and so
fucking arousing he almost embarrassed himself, almost sagged to his knees.

And then he kissed her back, maintaining eye contact, his fists tightly clenched at his sides to stop himself from taking what he wanted more than his next
breath. The kick of satisfaction he got from torturing
them both and withholding his touch tightened his balls,
ramping up his need until he feared he'd have to break
his word and gorge on her like a greedy, selfish addict.
Here. *Now.*

When she pushed her tongue into his mouth, whimpering her frustration and pressing her body against the length of his, he gave up the fight with a groan of both frustration and surrender. His fingers gripped the soft cheeks of her arse, lifting her and pressing her where he needed to feel friction. So close, but not close enough.

He spun her around, pressing her into the mirrored wall of the lift and crushing his steel-hard erection into the flat of her belly.

She deepened the kiss, her mouth voracious, as if she hadn't been kissed in a very long time. A travesty, if it were true. She deserved to be kissed every second of every day.

He snaked one hand towards the hem of her skirt, now regretting that it hugged her curves so tightly. He'd have to work to peel it up her legs, raise it high enough to part her thighs, hoist her above the gleaming chrome handrail that ran around the lift at waist height. Need raged through him, weakening his knees and making his hands rough, impatient. He tempered the roar of hormones spiking his blood with deep breaths.

Slow. Savour.

The lift pinged, announcing their arrival. Neither of them seemed in any hurry to break the searing kiss that had left their chests rising and falling in unison. Alex used every ounce of strength he possessed to pull back, pushing her skirt down just before the door slid open.

The corridor was deserted.

Without a backward glance, although looking a little flustered, Libby led the way to her room. Alex swiped the card she'd given him in the bar. Her eyes—huge dark pools in the dim lighting of the corridor—beguiled him. His blind confidence wavered. He was used to commanding every aspect of his life, and this power exchange, while exciting, left him adrift. Would he be able to concede to her wishes, whatever they were? For more of her, he'd certainly die trying.

But curiosity won.

'What do you want?'

He'd promised her a compromise, give and take, control. He'd do everything in his power to give her what she needed.

She pushed inside the room, flipping on lights and kicking of her heels, revealing toes painted with deep red nail polish.

As the door snicked closed behind him she turned.

He'd been right. Their kisses had left her mouth gloriously swollen, and the slight flush of beard burn marked her chin and cheeks. She was more beautiful than ever, and his fingers itched to complete the transformation—to undo her hair, currently featuring in all his filthy fantasies, and strip her of her prim clothes, expose the soft, feminine curves he guessed lurked beneath.

When she finally found her voice, it was so smoky he expected it to trigger the fire alarms.

'What do *you* want?'

That was easy to answer. A dream come true. 'I want to touch you. All of you.' He curled his fingers into his palms, his breath trapped behind his tight throat.

She nodded, eyes heavy, the tip of her tongue touching her top lip. '*I* want you to sit there.' She indicated an armchair in the corner by the windows.

He nodded, but his feet seemed cemented to the carpet while his mind played catch-up. He'd showed his hand too eagerly. She planned to deny him. Could he handle this? He burned for her, and the chair she'd indicated might as well be some sort of medieval torture device or wired to the mains.

She swallowed, her colour high. But it was not the flush of embarrassment, rather the glow of arousal.

'I want you to watch me.'

Fuck. She was trying to kill him. He was about to become a statistic. His throat closed tighter, his heart beating itself an escape path between his ribs.

'I want that too.' His voice was seriously strangled. *Get a grip, man.*

He shrugged off his blazer and tossed it on the desk. His jeans were too tight, constricting his manhood, but he'd do what she asked, what he'd agreed to, in order to earn her trust. Olivia—enchanting, provocative, intriguing—was the ultimate reward and certainly worth the discomfort.

He settled, sinking back into the upholstery, thighs spread as wide as the chair would allow. His hard-on was a stiff rod, pressing at the fly of his jeans. He forced his fingers to uncurl, resting them on the arms of the chair as he tried to slow his excited breaths. Whatever she was about to do would slay him. But he'd die trying to maintain the boundaries she'd demanded.

His compliance was quickly rewarded. She undid the top few buttons of her silky blouse, revealing the spill of perfect breasts over the top of a lacy, pale peach bra. His eyes fought not to roll back in his head. He wouldn't miss one second of the vision before him.

Her chest rose and fell in cadence with his own. At least they were in this together. Suffering together.

Staring him down, she hoisted up her skirt, bunching the fabric around her waist until her matching panties came into view at the juncture of her long, shapely legs. Her hands trembled slightly. If he hadn't been watching her every move with almost frantic eyes, desperate to see everything, he might have missed that revelation.

Was she nervous? Excited? Having second thoughts?

Pain lanced his chest.

Please don't regret this. Please don't stop.

Fuck, she was a wet dream come true. Somehow this tease was twice as hot as if she'd stripped naked.

But he didn't have to wait long to see more of her. With a small sigh, she hooked her thumbs into the waistband of those panties and peeled them down her legs, dropping them without ceremony and settling on the edge of the bed.

She faced him, vulnerable but still in control. Breathtaking, but still composed. Time slowed, stretching to infinity while he watched and waited and breathed.

'Don't move or I'll stop,' she whispered.

A nod. He was incapable of speech.

Just when he thought he'd shatter if he didn't kiss her, touch her soon, she slid her thighs open. He tried to keep his stare fixed on hers, but he wasn't the man he prided himself on being, because with a hissed *'Fuck...'* he capitulated to his body's needs, his eyes zeroing in on the patch of dark curls and her glistening sex.

She was wet. Soaked.

Two or three feet. That was all that separated them.

In one stride he'd be there, touching her slick heat, kissing her gasps away, feeling the scrape of her nails as he worked her to orgasm.

His own nails, blunt and useless, dug into the chair's fabric, his knuckles tight with the force of staying put. His breath see-sawed through flared nostrils, and his mouth pressed into a grim line as he lifted desperate eyes to hers once more.

She'd clearly decided he would comply, because with an aching slowness that tested every scrap of his substantial self-control she moved her hand between her legs, her fingers sliding into place over her clit.

A slug of lust punched him in the chest.

She gasped, her head falling back as if she was as close as him to slamming over the edge. She licked her lower lip, sultry eyes on him, and shifted, bent one leg up on the bed and braced the other on the floor, opening up the view to him.

His cock strained, begging for release. He gripped the armrests tighter, clinging to prevent himself from ripping open his fly and joining her in self-pleasure. But she'd told him to sit, to watch, and this was the most erotic thing he'd ever witnessed.

His breathing, now perilously fast, echoed around the room.

She moved her hand slowly at first, tentatively, as if she'd forgotten the rhythm of pleasuring herself. Or perhaps she'd never done this before. Perhaps she was as blown away by her bold, uninhibited display as he was. *Fuck*. The thought of some other lucky bastard being treated to this show forced icy shards through his chest and he bit his tongue, the pain reminding him to stay seated when every nerve in his body relayed messages to his brain to move. To go to her.

As her fingers picked up speed he lost his grip on sanity, his stare darting wildly between her pleasure-drunk face and her frantically circling fingers. She dropped back on her elbow, the edges of her blouse slipping open, revealing more of the lacy concoction concealing her breasts.

He gritted his teeth. He resented her clothing now. It blocked what he instinctively knew would be a sublime body from his view. He made fists, the urge to tear the fabric from her curves so overwhelming his legs shifted, restless with inactivity.

Her whimpers drew his gaze to her face, but his eyes flew back between her legs in time to see her slide a finger inside herself before returning to her clit. He'd been right. She was soaked. The quiet noise of slippery skin on slippery skin echoed inside his skull and her scent, rich and erotic, reached his nostrils across the small space separating them.

He was losing it. His brain was shutting down. Not enough oxygen. Too much stimulation. Testosterone overload.

She stared at him, her moans growing increasingly erratic. Breath catching. Lips parting. Thighs jerking.

She was close.

He was done.

With a powerful lurch he flew from the chair, his whole body rejoicing, joining his addled mind until his head filled with triumphant screams. He fell to his knees between her thighs, his focus zeroed in on her sex.

He'd assumed she'd stop. That was her rule. But clearly she was as gone as him—well past the point of no return. Well past reason.

He looked up…a moment's hesitation.

She whimpered. Gave a single nod. Desperation in her eyes.

Batting her still moving hand aside, he slammed his mouth over her slick folds with a grunt, glorying in the euphoria of touching her at last.

She yelled—a cry of ecstasy—twisting her fingers in his hair.

He groaned out his pent-up frustration. Her taste coated his lips, his tongue, the back of his throat. He located the hard, swollen nub of nerves, flicking wildly with the tip of his tongue before sucking down on her— hard.

He stared up from between her legs. Her head thrashed from side to side as she watched him, her cries growing louder, more primitive. He managed to push a single finger inside her tight warmth just before she exploded, her internal muscles a contracting wave around his finger and her thighs trembling against the sides of his face. He kept his mouth glued in place, wringing the last spasms from her, while the uneasy swirl of triumph and failure stole his high.

With a final gasp she twisted away, pushing at his head when only seconds ago she'd been pulling.

He released her, wiping his mouth on the back of his hand and staggering to his feet. His cock was harder than ever. She lay on the bed, boneless, her beautiful face flushed with the aftermath of intense pleasure, but her eyes were wide and wary, as if she was uncertain what he'd do next.

Fuck. He'd failed. She'd set him a test and he'd bombed spectacularly. Now he wished she'd tied him to that chair—although he couldn't be sure he wouldn't have torn the building down, trying to get to her. The sight of her had been too much for the mere mortal he'd proved to be.

He held out his hands, their fine tremors matching the adrenaline jitters pounding the rest of his body. For a second he thought she'd refuse. Tell him to get out. But she struggled into a sitting position, put her hands in his, allowing him to pull her up so that he stood between her knees where she sat on the edge of the bed, dishevelled and breathtaking.

Slowly, as though coaxing a frightened animal, he cupped her face. Her hair, still in its ponytail, was less than immaculate, with freed wisps clinging to her forehead and cheeks. Her eyes had lost their unfocussed haze, and pleasure was draining away to be replaced by a wariness that shrank his balls.

This hadn't been part of the game—wasn't in the rulebook. He'd messed up.

He released a sigh—slow, controlled, careful not to expel all his frustration in one explosive blast. He bent over her, eyes fixed on hers, and placed a single, firm, closed-mouth kiss on her lips. The effort of withdrawing almost buckled his knees, but he dropped her face and stepped back.

She'd been perfect. Given him everything she'd said she would. Given him an experience that he'd remember on his deathbed. And he'd failed her. At the first hurdle.

Without a word he turned away, his back on fire, urging him to look at her again. But as the heavy hotel door closed behind him and he made his way to the lift on legs with the potential to let him down at any second, he congratulated himself. He might have fallen short, let her down. But he was damn proud of the hidden strength that allowed him to walk away.

CHAPTER FOUR

LIBBY'S SCALP REBELLED. She'd pulled her hair into a severe braid this morning, as if an austere hairstyle might protect her from the reckless impulses of last night. Impulses that had not only had her agreeing to work with Alex Lancaster, but to stay in London for a week when she'd planned to be back in New York in two days.

Not to mention the crazy tit-for-tat deal they'd brokered—the one in which she'd pleasured herself in front of him, forced him to watch, and come so hard she was certain her heart had stopped for a beat.

She stepped from the elevator, the chafe of her stocking tops grazing her thighs, which were already embarrassingly slick.

She'd almost cancelled. Called his PA. Booked an earlier flight home. She wasn't a coward, but the thought of what she'd done, of seeing Alex again in the cold light of day…

Whilst last night's antics had blown her away with the best orgasm of her life, she'd be lying if she said she and Alex had concluded their business—either with Able-Active or in the personal game they'd begun.

His face flashed before her. He'd kept his word. Conceded control. Hadn't once balked at her demands. She'd never have guessed a man as powerful and influential as him would be able to shelve his arrogance and give her what she needed. And now what had started as a battle of wills, a way to deal with her lust for him, had become the most daring and exhilarating game ever.

Not that she'd expected him to follow her instructions to the letter. She had almost sobbed with relief when he'd prowled from the chair and finished her off with his mouth. She closed her eyes, remembering the sight of him looking up at her from between her thighs.

How had he managed to walk away unfulfilled? She'd been on the verge of running after him, dragging him back to her room and riding his magnificent-looking cock. Not that she'd had a chance to get her hands on him. He'd barely broken a sweat. The man had some frustratingly impressive willpower. She'd just have to try harder.

But business first.

Libby pushed through etched glass doors emblazoned with the company logo and approached a sleek, minimalist reception desk.

'Libby Noble for Alex Lancaster.'

Late last night, after showering, she'd checked her e-mails, spying one from his PA, Molly—the young woman now sitting in front of her, according to a name plaque on the desk—advising her of today's itinerary.

'Ah, yes, Ms Noble. He's expecting you. I'll show you in.' Molly stood, her outstretched arm directing

Libby towards another set of etched glass doors and an office beyond.

Her legs threatened to give out. She swallowed, plastered her most convincing, polite smile on her face and steeled herself against the impact of seeing Alex again—steeled herself like a butterfly about to enter a hurricane.

He stood at his desk, shoulder to shoulder with a shorter man in his forties. Their focus was directed to the screen of the tablet the other man carried, but as she hovered in the doorway Alex lifted his head, harpooning Libby with a dark, inscrutable stare across the space that divided them.

A flush of heat slammed through her, and the hurricane morphed into a tropical cyclone on the surface of the sun. She'd been right to fear the impact. It hadn't lessened.

Even though she'd broken her dry spell, achieved some measure of relief from the sexual haze she'd been in since meeting him, the blow was twice as potent as the first time their eyes had met across a room.

She saw him now. The true him. Her eyes had been cleared of the self-imposed veil of abstinence. His raw sexuality simmered beneath his cultured, polite exterior. He stripped her with his stare, leaving her aching and needy and desperate to sample more of him than his spectacular mouth.

Libby swayed on her heels—a minute wobble in his direction that told her everything she needed to know about her chances of her steering her mind out of the bedroom and into the boardroom. No amount of prim business suits or severe hairstyles could protect her from Alex's potent sex appeal and her body's awakened cravings.

From behind her, Molly cleared her throat. 'Ms Noble.'

Of course—they weren't alone.

Alex gave a single nod to his assistant. 'Thanks, Molly.'

The older man moved into Libby's peripheral vision.

Alex kept his eyes on her. 'Olivia, this is Jeremy Wells, my financial director.'

Jeremy tucked the tablet under his arm and moved in her direction.

Dragging her thoughts and her eyes from Alex, Libby smiled, heat warming her cheeks from her transparent leering at Jeremy's boss.

Get a grip.

Alex sat on the edge of his desk, observing their interaction with an indifference that sent an army of ants marching beneath her skin.

'Olivia will be in charge of marketing for Able-Active.'

His voice held none of the sexy drawl of last night, but the way his mouth caressed her name reverberated through her body until she felt the memory of that mouth's intimate caress between her legs. A memory constantly at the forefront of her mind.

Jeremy offered a surprisingly limp handshake and a tepid smile. 'I'll leave you to your business.'

Alex nodded again, his stare back on Libby, flooding her body with wave after wave of turbulent heat.

But she'd yet to see what she wanted to see—the same aching discord currently pounding *her* equilibrium.

Hormones. It was just hormones.

'Molly, could you please bring coffee downstairs?' He quirked an eyebrow at Libby in question.

She nodded to the younger woman, confirming that he'd guessed her beverage of choice.

'I'm taking Ms Noble on a tour of the Able-Active office.'

Molly nodded and retreated, seemingly completely unaffected by the decadent rumble of her boss's voice, whereas Libby felt it wash over her, lifting every hair and tingling every nerve ending.

She wanted more of it. More of the sexy grunts and groans he'd uttered last night from between her thighs. More of him asking her what she wanted, handing her control on a silver platter. More of his buttoned-up English accent cursing as he finally reached his limit of self-denial and lunged for her.

Who knew this part of her lurked inside? What had he unleashed?

They faced off, alone at last. He gave nothing away. She prayed her own transparency matched his. Would he renege on their deal? Send her home? Perhaps he'd simply pretend last night hadn't happened and get straight down to business?

Not that he was dressed for business. She indulged herself, eyeing him from head to toe. She'd expected another of his expensive suits, to see his magnificent body encased in fine tailoring and crisp linen, but he wore jeans and a graphic T-shirt—an outfit that did nothing to diminish his attractiveness. If anything, it heightened it, and the T-shirt was a playful touch of whimsy that almost curled her lip in a smile. Alex Lancaster a gamer? She'd been right about the geeky surfer dude.

She lifted her stare from the casual, low-slung fit of his jeans, which showcased the bulge of his crotch. A bulge considerably smaller than the one he'd walked away with last night, when he'd left her hotel room unsatisfied. Fresh heat climbed her neck. She should have stopped him. Given him some relief. Finished him the way he'd finished her.

Her knees wobbled at the memory of his mouth on her, those dark eyes piercing, watching while she exploded on his tongue...

Damn. Must she eye-fuck him at every opportunity?

Her face burned. But the intensity of the look he gave her provided little respite from the boil of her blood.

The speech she'd prepared fled. She scanned the room rather that look at him, while her brain scrambled for suitable morning-after conversation—the spectacular view of the London skyline, the tasteful, minimalist art on the walls and the rich aroma of leather from the expensive furniture.

When her gaze ended its tour back on him, he continued to watch her with slightly narrowed eyes.

'I wasn't sure you'd turn up this morning.'

That was the last thing she'd expected him to say. *Fancy a repeat performance? Want to lean over my desk while I fuck you from behind? You're a selfish lover and the deal is off.* All those were closer to her imaginings.

'Why? I agreed. I'm a professional.'

Sometimes. When she wasn't drooling over him.

She was a big girl—one who could separate personal from business. Not that she'd ever been tested before now. Oh, how she hoped her faith in her own abilities was justified.

Liar.

Right now, all she wanted to do was strip him from his dressed-down street clothes and see if she could make him hard with just her mouth.

His expression inscrutable, his eyes flicked over her face and he stood. 'Shall we?'

He moved to the door, holding it open and gesturing her to re-enter the real world. So calm. So indifferent.

Clearly they weren't going to discuss last night. Discuss the inferno of chemistry they'd fanned to life. Only her mind was stuck there. Stuck on vivid images of him splaying her over his desk, his sofa, the floor, and continuing where they left off in her hotel room.

But Mr Lancaster was all business this morning. And that was where her head belonged. In the game. The game of marketing for Able-Active and the game of bedroom *quid pro quo*. She wouldn't become professionally distracted from the first and she *couldn't* become personally distracted by the second.

She crossed his office, her eyes flicking up to his as she passed him in the doorway, and headed back the way she'd come to the elevators. He walked beside her, his arm so close she could reach out and touch him. Perhaps she should. Apologise for last night. For leaving him…hanging. Suggest they rectify the imbalance of the situation later tonight.

He pressed the call button and they both gazed up. The feeling of *déjà vu* was strong enough to send licks of flame trickling down Libby's spine. Just like last night, the elevator was empty. Alex pressed the button for a few floors down and the doors closed.

The crackle of tension ricocheted around inside Libby's head. She craved more of those searing, all-consuming kisses. *Damn*, the man could kiss, and she'd already experienced his phenomenal oral skills. But instead of dispelling her torrid urges it had only intensified them. She wanted to stop the elevator and beg him to fuck her right here, right now.

Her eyes scanned the interior of the car, searching for security cameras.

And then the doors slid open, and his upper-class voice dragged her from her fantasies.

'After you.'

Seriously? She could barely walk. Her nipples ached, her panties were ruined and her fingers twitched to get hold of him. She should have asked him to spend the night—that way she could have quenched her thirst with the perfect wake-up call this morning.

Alex, by comparison, seemed calm, efficient and businesslike. The ultimate professional. While she longed to play hooky with him, forget marketing budgets and brand awareness strategies and spend the week holed up in her hotel room, living out every dirty fantasy he'd inspired.

No. He'd definitely changed his mind. A cold, hard rock settled in her stomach.

He led her down a corridor that was a carbon copy of the one housing his office, again holding open the door for her to enter ahead of him when they reached their destination.

Libby stalled. 'Office' was a fairly grand term for what was essentially a small room with two desks, a single computer and a phone.

A woman in her early twenties looked up from the screen and stood on their arrival. 'Hi, Alex.'

First-name terms? Of course.

He smiled, and Libby glanced away.

'Hailey, this is Olivia Noble. She's agreed to help with our marketing campaign. Put us on the map.'

He turned to Libby, the smile for his pretty young employee sliding from his face.

'Hailey is the charity's only full-time employee. The rest of the staff are volunteers.'

Libby shook hands with the woman, noting the way her eyes lingered on Alex. She didn't blame her. 'Magnetic' didn't really cover his appeal. And her resentment of Hailey, a woman she'd just met, originated in disappointment. He hadn't brought her to this quiet part of the building for a repeat performance of last night. He wouldn't be laying her over this desk and redressing the orgasm imbalance.

Damn.

If they'd been alone she might have broken her number one rule. Might have dropped to her knees in front of him, taken him in her mouth, given him something other than work to think about.

'Any progress on the mountain biking trip?'

Alex took a folder from Hailey's desk, his eyes scanning the contents.

Libby shook the tantalising images from her head. She could do indifference too.

Hailey nodded. 'Some luck with the accommodation, thanks to the Welsh Tourism Board, but staffing is still an issue.'

Alex traced his bottom lip with his finger and thumb, his attention held by the paperwork in his hands.

Olivia cast her observant eye around the sparsely furnished and featureless room. One employee, an uninspiring space and staffing issues—hardly the picture of a successful Alex Lancaster venture. Why devote so much of his time to a fledgling charity? Time he could spend in more lucrative ways, building his empire. Surely Lancaster IT kept him busy?

With conversation clearly over, Libby followed Alex to the room's spare desk, where he pulled out a chair for her before taking the second and moving it so they sat at right angles, rather than facing each other. *Damn.* She'd hoped a block of wood between them would coax her hormones into submission, or at least remind her to stay professional.

She busied herself with her tablet and her phone and then slid off her jacket, draping it over her bag at her feet.

Cool, calm, professional.

Right.

Her thighs still felt the imprint of that stubble he wore on his chin.

His low voice penetrated the lust filling her head as they faced off.

'Are you okay? You seem…uncomfortable.'

Damn him—how dare he be so…unaffected? Her gaze flicked down. At least her hands weren't trembling.

'Not at all. I…'

She couldn't confess the real direction of her lewd thoughts. Him. This desk. More orgasms good enough to make her forget her own name. Time for Plan B. Her trusty go-to—honesty.

'I'm a little surprised, that's all.'

He leaned back in his chair as he had last night in that armchair. A lazy slouch, thighs spread, one eyebrow cocked…waiting.

How was she going to get through today?

She squirmed, swallowing hard, then pointed around the room. 'I guess I expected something…*more*. Something flashier.' She clasped her hands on the desk in front of her.

He was silent for so long, she felt beads of moisture dotting her top lip. Silent and watchful.

'I see.'

He hardened his stare and Libby fought the urge to hide in the restroom. *Fuck*, was it possible that work Alex was even hotter than play Alex? He certainly carried an intense air of authority she hadn't witnessed before. One that should leave her cold, and angling for a heated debate, but it only heightened the ache between her legs.

'You've made assumptions about me…developed preconceived ideas.' He held up his hand, silencing the denial on the tip of her tongue. 'The scruffy jeans and T-shirt have thrown you, and now this slightly shabby low-tech office has compounded those impressions.'

Haughty. The word perfectly described his cold voice. *Had* she made assumptions? She tried to remain open-minded, unbiased—especially where business was concerned. But with her humble past and his reckless reputation… An oil-and-water combination. Perhaps she'd subconsciously doomed this opportunity to failure. And if that were true there'd be no more… recreation.

She fought the weight on her shoulders.

He leaned closer, capturing her rapt stare and holding her breath to ransom. 'I told you on the phone yesterday—Able-Active doesn't happen in an office.'

Her eyes landed on his mouth. The hypnotic movement and the sound of his passionate voice were entrancing, luring her back into sensual waters. Waters that lapped at her, bringing every nerve ending screaming back to life.

'It's about adventure.' His gaze dipped to her mouth. 'Thrill. Adrenaline.'

His lips caressed every word as they'd caressed her clit, and the phantom tingles there reminded her how good it had been.

Were they still talking about the charity?

If the hot billionaire and his business proposal had had her panting, this passionate philanthropist with his sleeves rolled up would suffocate her. How would it feel to be the focus of all that...*passion*?

He continued while her brain reeled, trying to untangle his words from her overactive imagination.

'Just because our clients are intellectually-disabled teens and young adults, it doesn't mean they don't want the same things from life that any other teen wants.' A shrug. 'That any of us wants.'

He leaned back in his seat and Libby's heart stuttered back to life.

His finger and thumb traced his bottom lip in that way of his—a sign of deep contemplation. 'Everyone deserves to experience that kind of...*rush*.'

She shivered, convinced he was referring to last night and her display. But he'd said nothing, done nothing even remotely inappropriate. It was *her* mind stuck in the gutter. *Her* mind choreographing a repeat performance of that rush he'd described so eloquently.

Alex steered her wayward thoughts back to business. 'Have you visited the UK before?'

Libby cleared her throat, pressing her thighs together. 'No. This is my first visit.' What was *wrong* with her? Last night should have cured her of this fervid need crawling beneath her skin.

He nodded. Stared. 'Let me show you what we have so far and where I'd like us to be in six months.'

His voice had snapped out of that low, confessional tone, was brisk and businesslike again. He flipped open the folder, forcing her attention away from him.

By the end of the morning he'd outlined his vision

for the charity and, despite her best attempts at professionalism, Libby was as sexually frustrated as ever.

'Up?' Libby quizzed Alex.

His brief, decisive nod gave little away. When he'd suggested lunch she'd refused, preferring to work through and grab something later—alone—allowing herself some distance from his perplexing proximity. But he'd made a persuasive argument, stating that he'd missed breakfast, and her loud, rumbling stomach had chosen that precise moment to announce that she had too.

He nodded, those dark eyes cryptic, penetrating. All morning, he'd kept his hands to himself, never once touching her, as if he was maintaining a professional line and refusing to cross it. While *she'd* lusted and leered, ashamed of the lewd direction of her thoughts. Clearly he was more adept at separating business from pleasure. Or maybe, as far as he was concerned, they were through.

The slow simmer that gripped her every time she looked at him or thought about him drained away, leaving chills in its place.

After a beat, he said, 'Pinot Gris or Sauvignon Blanc?'

The elevator arrived, interrupting her answer, which was still forming from the scramble of her thoughts. He ushered her inside, his hand finally finding the small of her back—the first time he'd touched her since his mouth had left her last night. The zing of electricity was so strong she expected to find her panties singed.

All morning she'd battled to stay professional while craving his touch. As he'd waxed lyrical about the Able-Active team, their inspirational clients and the multitude of ideas he had to expand their scope nationally, she'd fought to drag her eyes away from his animated features, lit up with an enthusiasm that had left her envious. Envious of his colleagues, who probably saw this side of him daily. Envious of his beloved clients, who inspired such heartfelt passion. And envious of the women who'd experienced that intensity transformed into a different kind of focus—one she craved like the next lungful of oxygen.

What had he asked her? Wine...

She lifted her chin, determined to appear as unaffected as him. 'I prefer Pinot Gris, but I don't mind. I'll probably pass.'

The last thing she needed was to add alcohol to the heady mix of hormones and endorphins bubbling through her blood. Any further lowering of her inhibitions in Alex's presence and she'd start clawing at his clothes in public. How could he be so unruffled?

But was she imagining the tension that built inside the elevator? He stood so close she could almost feel the tickle of the dark hairs on his arm, and the clean, soapy scent of him wafted over her on a cloud of warmth.

The air thickened as the car ascended. Libby locked her knees; scared she might sway towards him, throw herself into his arms or just simply press the emergency stop button and strip.

'I thought you said lunch? Is there a restaurant in this building?'

It looked just like a typical office block. Still, this was his city. She merely hoped they'd arrive at their floor soon, so she could put some more space between them. Or persuade him to fuck her in the restroom...

'I'm taking you to a restaurant I own. The Pinot Gris there is world-class.' His gaze dipped to her mouth, his tongue swiping his bottom lip.

Was he thinking about wine, or tasting her?

'You can allow yourself one glass, surely?'

His mouth curled. Was he daring her? He'd lost some of that morning's surliness, and his eyes danced with gold flecks. To say she'd missed relaxed, playful Alex would be an understatement. But she admired his ability to compartmentalise—a skill she normally shared.

The car juddered to a halt, its doors opening to another bland, deserted corridor.

Where was he taking her? Was she about to become a murder statistic?

Hysterical laughter threatened—a side effect of too much adrenaline.

At the end of the corridor Alex swiped a card through a lock and held the door open for Libby. The narrow concrete stairs were draughty, and the height from the windows spun her head and flipped her stomach into her throat, pushing the thought of wine and even lunch far from her mind.

Alex took her hand and pushed open a fire door, escorting her onto the roof.

Her feet stalled.

No rooftop restaurant with views of the Thames.

No murderer's lair.

Just a helicopter.

Gripping her waist, he ushered her frozen with shock form towards the sleek white death trap.

She dug her heels into the concrete, skidding them to a standstill. 'I'm not going in that.'

His brow dipped, puzzlement cloaking his amused eyes. 'Of course you are. It's only a thirty-minute ride.' He cocked a brow, his mouth twisted in challenge. 'You'll love it.'

In two strides he'd opened the door, was holding out his arm, enticing her inside a form of transportation she'd never experienced and never wanted to.

The wind whipped loosened strands of hair across her face, blinding her. Her stomach fell, settling somewhere behind her wobbling knees. The height of this building alone was enough to drain her adrenal glands. Just like at The Shard yesterday, being inside this skyscraper was enough of a trial for her, let alone standing on top of it with the elements determined to send her plummeting to the ground.

He strode back to her side, face contrite and eyes soft. 'Olivia. I'm sorry.'

He reached for her cold hand, his warm fingers clasping. She clung to the lifeline, some of her fear dissipating at his touch.

'I should have warned you instead of trying to surprise you.' His thumb rubbed the back of her hand.

Her fickle mind switched. Now she prayed for the release of a ground-swallowing demise. She hated anyone seeing this weak side of her, but especially Alex. Fearless, sophisticated Alex, who thought nothing of jumping into a helicopter for lunch at his favourite restaurant.

He was still talking, still cajoling. She forced herself to hear him over the ringing in her ears.

'It's very safe. Weather conditions are perfect. I have thousands of hours in the air and that Pinot really is worth it, I promise.'

Her belly flopped again. She glanced down at her stiletto-clad toes, almost expecting to see it there on the concrete. Decision time. Ride in a helicopter or get blown from the roof? Accept his challenge or admit defeat and concede the bargaining chip? It was a close one.

She willed her breathing into submission as her mind dithered. At least he'd dropped the cocky smirks of moments ago and the hard, inscrutable stares present all morning and seemed genuinely concerned.

As if he'd made the decision for her, he turned back towards the door to the stairway. 'Okay. I'm sorry. I was wrong. We'll go somewhere else for lunch.'

He slid his arm around her shoulders, as if guiding a child or an old lady safely across the road.

'No.' Her declaration surprised both of them. 'I'll go.'

What was she saying? She didn't need to impress him. She could admit she'd prefer not to put her life in the hands of a man she barely knew inside a chunk of flying metal. There'd be no shame in that. He didn't need to know why she had an aversion to death traps, or to anything she considered risky. It was an aversion founded in past experience—one that had changed her life for ever.

No. That labyrinth of sickening memories wasn't going to help her get off this roof with her dignity intact.

'You sure? There's no pressure.'

He pushed a stray wisp of hair behind her ear, his eyes tracing her features but his fingertips failing to make contact.

'We'll do whatever you want.' His voice was low, sincere, calming.

The echo of those words from last night reminded her of the power she held. It surged through her veins, dispelling fear, forcing steel into her skeleton and redirecting her thoughts from all things death-related.

Latching on to her attraction for him, she blurted out the thought that had occupied most of her mind since the minute she'd walked into his office that morning.

'I want you to kiss me.'

In an instant his face hardened, as if she'd slapped him. She swallowed, her cheeks hot. *Why* had she said that? If the deal was off, their sexual exploration over, she'd just set herself up for rejection.

Rejection and humiliation all in one morning—way to go, Libby.

Her gaze fell to his crotch, saw the bulge there expanding before her eyes.

No. He was still in this with her. The chemistry was still alive. She straightened her spine, the surge of power, of control, imbuing her limbs with courage.

'Kiss me and I'll go.'

Wow—pushy, much? But she was already so far out of her comfort zone she'd need a map to locate it again. She might as well get what she wanted from this situation.

He dropped his hands to his sides and made fists, his fingers flexing. Still trying to keep things professional? Acting the gentleman? Having second thoughts?

She took a half-step closer until his clean, soapy scent reached her, giving her a head rush that had nothing to with dizzying heights or stomach-dropping rides.

'Kiss me like you're telling me that you wanted to fuck me last night instead of leaving.'

Please—before she came to her senses and fled, or passed out.

His nostrils flared as he sucked in a harsh breath, focussed his intense stare on hers.

'I did.'

His voice, full of gravel, scraped her raw—as raw as the hunger she saw flare in his eyes.

'I did want to fuck you last night. You told me to watch.'

Yes. She'd got what she wanted—but the hollow victory had left her cold.

He closed the gap between them by another half step. 'I can't get the taste of you out of my mouth.' His gaze flicked down, scorching her from head to toe. 'The image of you lying there, your hand working between your legs…'

He dropped his head back, closing his eyes for a second before he pinned her with his penetrating stare once more.

'Believe me, I've wanted to kiss you all fucking morning.'

His admission knocked the air from her lungs, and a surge of triumph banished the last of her doubts.

'Why don't you then?' Barely a whisper.

His lips thinned, air gusting out of flared nostrils. 'Fucked if I know.'

They reached for each other, closing the distance with a lurch. He slammed his mouth over hers and she practically jumped up to meet him. His arms locked around her waist to catch her in mid-air. Her fingers delved into his hair as he pressed her close, their mouths opening and tongues sliding with ravenous need. The icy fear of moments ago trickled away, replaced by the sluggish thrill of euphoria. Her limbs liquefied, and the thud of her heart was loud enough to block out all her reservations.

Yes. This was what she'd craved since last night. The knowledge that she wasn't alone in her furious attraction to this man. He felt it too. Their searing connection. The all-consuming rush. The need to feed the fire with any available fuel.

They pulled back, breath gusting.

Alex gripped her face, his eyes darting between hers. 'You sure?'

She couldn't speak. His concern, his consideration in the wake of that kiss was too much.

She nodded. Another stomach flip—although she couldn't tell if it was fear this time or the heady knowledge that there'd be more of those kisses if she wanted them. More of *him*.

He slid his hands from her face, one capturing her hand. Warm, confident, his grip was firm and comforting. With a single resolute nod that filled her with belief in his piloting skills he turned them back towards the helicopter.

But for all her bravado and bravery, the clack of her heels on the concrete roof echoed.

A death march or the soundtrack to an adventure?

CHAPTER FIVE

'TOLD YOU IT was worth it.'

Alex eyed her over the rim of his wine glass. The early-evening sun glinted off her dark hair, revealing glowing streaks of gold. The same gold streaks that flashed in her eyes when she challenged him, berated him or when she was turned on.

How quickly he'd grown to crave those flashes—a sure sign that he'd got to her, whether to rile up her keen mind and razor-sharp wit or to witness the unapologetic hunger that mirrored his own. Despite the professional business attire and the way she tamed her hair, Olivia claimed her sexuality as she owned her forthright manner and articulate negotiation skills.

She put her glass to her lips and his eyes were mesmerised by their plump curves and the tiny flash of pink tongue.

She swallowed, shrugging one elegant shoulder. 'It's okay. I've had better. Californian wines are the best in the world.'

At least her acidic sense of humour had returned, along with the colour in her cheeks. *Fuck*, what an idiot

he'd been. He should have *asked* her, rather than assumed she'd be happy to fly. His bird was his favourite mode of transportation. And some primitive part
of his brain had wanted to impress her with a flashy
stunt. A dick move.

But he'd made good on his promise. The flight to his
Oxfordshire boutique winery and restaurant had lasted
only thirty minutes. She'd even managed to open her eyes
for long enough to enjoy the views, and a begrudging,
tight smile had hovered on her beautiful mouth.

As soon as they'd landed he'd ushered her to the
Thames-side restaurant on his estate, where the glass
of wine had been chilled and waiting for her on the best
table in the house.

She placed her glass back on the table, her eyes scanning the three-Michelin-starred restaurant. Two or three
other parties occupied tables in the conservatory, which
was decorated with a sea of twinkling fairy lights that
bounced shards of light off the silver dinnerware and
the crisp snow-white table linen.

'So *this* is how you impress women?'

He laughed. She slayed him. The twitch of her mouth
and the haughty tilt of her chin let him know that she
was far from affected by him *or* his lifestyle. Her poise,
her cutting wit, her acerbic tongue, her uncompromising
cut-to-the-chase attitude—all of it made him want to put
on airs and graces just to rile her up and see that flash in
her eyes and the dismissive shake of her head. Why was
sparring with her such a turn-on?

'I don't usually have to work so hard. And now I'm
curious as to why you're so impervious.'

What would it take to impress her? A prize certainly worth having.

Her eyes hardened and he discreetly adjusted his ever-present erection.

'Is that what this is about? You show me your chopper and I fall at your grape-crushing feet? You'll have to pay better attention if you're expecting me to gush over your clever piloting skills.'

She opened the heavy embossed menu, lifting her nose and focussing her attention on the contents.

The flutter of her pulse at the base of her elegant neck gave her away and he shifted in his seat. *Fuck.* She turned him to steel—a pretty constant state and a bloody uncomfortable way to walk around. But he wasn't complaining. The throb reminded him of the deal they'd brokered, adding a fresh slug of adrenaline to course through his bloodstream.

Two of his favourite things. The heady thrill of a business negotiation and the buzz of exhilaration just before you jumped from the cliff's edge.

And the prize? Not only had this feisty, independent brunette agreed to lend her experience to his fledgling charity, she'd also instigated a game of control tag. A game that, as he saw it, he couldn't lose. A game that was still on, even though he'd disregarded her rules and gorged himself on her last night.

Not that he regretted that for one second. The memory of her taste was still potent enough to fog his mind.

His stomach growled. He was hungry for food, but even hungrier for her. That brief taste of her mouth on the roof of Lancaster Tower earlier had done little to quench his craving. He'd been hard since leaving her hotel room last night, his balls a heavy ache that he'd carried all day while she sat mere inches away, her scent tantalising, her luminous eyes seeing through him and her voice scraping over his nerve endings until he'd contemplated banging one out in his private bathroom like a randy teenager.

He'd forced himself not to touch her—determined to fight his attraction to her in case she called off the deal. He'd half expected her to bail, simply not to show up for their meeting. When she'd asked him to kiss her he'd thought he'd hallucinated. The urge to drag her into the helicopter, splay her over the leather seats and taste her again had been so powerful he'd had to bite the inside of his cheek until he'd tasted blood.

Watching her now, all elegant and poised, ignoring his attempts to wine and dine her and feigning absorption in the first-class menu, he wanted to scrap dinner and follow the commands from that dirty mouth of hers.

'I can recommend the filet mignon.' His lips twitched. 'The chef is a genius.'

He lounged back in his seat, enjoying the view of the slight flush at the base of her throat. What would that skin taste like? Better than any filet mignon—he'd bet his beloved helicopter on that.

She sniffed, her eyes trained on the menu. 'I'm a vegetarian.'

Damn. It irked him that he knew so little about her, an inconvenience he planned to rectify as soon as possible.

Why wait?

'Tell me something about yourself. Something I couldn't know from reading your business profile.' He stretched his legs out under the table, searching for hers.

She stared. 'Why?'

Her fingers clenched around the base of her wine glass. His probing had clearly raised her hackles.

He sipped his wine, enjoying her rising colour. 'Because we're not animals, Olivia. Our sexual chemistry is intense, but that doesn't mean we can't talk in between fucking. *Your* word, by the way.'

She shrugged, the pulse at her neck fluttering again, her smile sweet. 'I just did. I don't eat meat.'

Touché. Bewitching. He pressed his lips together.

'Tell me something about *you*,' she said. 'Something none of the women you've impressed has ever asked you.'

That, right there, was what intrigued him so much. She was so unexpected, unpredictable. She didn't give a damn about impressing him in return. She wasn't interested in learning his preferences so she could mould herself into what she thought would be his perfect woman.

Fine. He could be blunt too.

'No one's ever asked me to watch them pleasure themselves before.'

A hint of pink touched her cheekbones, but her stare remained bold, direct, captivating.

'Poor you.' She glanced back at menu, as if they'd discussed the weather.

Alex bit back his delight as the waiter arrived to take their order.

When they were alone again, she said, 'Why am I here? I appreciate the world-class dining experience, but you asked me to do a job—not to drink wine and eat truffle-infused mushrooms.'

He fought a smile. She cut straight to the chase, and her caustic turn of phrase... Did she *know* how much she turned him on?

'I did. A job you accepted with one mutually satisfying condition.'

The colour in her cheeks heightened. 'A job I could do perfectly adequately from my hotel room or even from New York.' Her eyes hardened.

He ran his index and middle fingers along his lower lip, studying her until she shifted in her seat, revealing an alluring glimpse of pert breasts in the V of her blouse.

Last night he'd seen dark nipples through the lace of her bra. He wanted her naked, to taste those nipples, to nibble, scrape and suck until she squirmed and writhed and perhaps even came. Would she be that responsive? Instinct told him *yes*.

He hardened his own stare. 'I thought we'd established the parameters of our working relationship?'

A little reminder of their deal. After all, if she intended to torture him as she had last night he'd push her boundaries in return. *Quid pro quo*.

At her silent scrutiny, he continued. 'I want you to fully experience what I have in mind for Able-Active. As I said this morning, you can't do that in an office.'

She wasn't buying it—was still looking at him as if he'd sprouted a second head.

'You need to experience the thrill. If the kids can do it, *we* can, right? You said yourself that the Able-Active headquarters is completely uninspiring.'

And he wanted to get her out of those elegant suits in more ways than one.

'What exactly will it involve?'

Wary eyes, darker than midnight.

He shrugged. 'Mountain biking, boating, kayaking, abseiling. You name it.'

Her brow pinched. 'Why? I don't need to hurl myself from a climbing wall to understand the concept.'

He clenched his jaw, pinning her with his stare. 'You agreed to stay a week. I agreed to your terms. Are you backing out of our deal?'

Fuck, had he pushed too hard? Was this over before it had begun?

She flushed, her eyes dipping to the crystal glassware. 'No. But I won't be blindsided either. If you expect me to participate I'll need advance warning.'

'Why? Spontaneity is more rewarding.'

As last night had proved. He hadn't intended to declare his hand. But the results…

A head-shake. Decisive and unyielding. 'Maybe for you.' Her chin lifted as she glared him down. '*I* like to plan.'

'Control?' His cock stirred again, remembering the last time she'd taken the lead.

A staring contest ensued, and the space between them sparked with tension. He was half tempted to cancel the food they'd ordered, clear the restaurant and hope her next demand would be that he fuck her on this very table, with the one-thousand-thread-count tablecloth clutched in her elegant hands as she came around him.

As if she knew his filthy thoughts she traced said tablecloth with her index finger. 'Let's say I *do* don a cycle helmet or a lifejacket. Couldn't we do all that in London? Why here?'

He sobered, his lips turning in while he chose his next words. 'I live here.' He flicked his head in the direction of the main house he'd pointed out from the helicopter. 'When I'm not in the city.'

He glanced down to where he rubbed the edge of his thick linen napkin between his thumb and forefinger, the hair rising at his nape as it always did when he was this close to his biggest vulnerability. Well, she'd wanted to know something about him no one else did.

'I wanted you to see this place.' When he looked up, he had her full attention. 'I have bigger plans for the charity. Bigger than I outlined to you today.'

A small nod, encouraging him to continue.

'Eventually I'd like Able-Active to have an employment arm. The statistics on unemployment in the disabled population are depressing.'

He shifted in his chair, forcing his voice to remain even, although this topic of conversation usually led to gut-wrenching impotence.

'I'd like the winery here, the hotel, perhaps even Lancaster IT, to broaden its sphere. Improve on its equal opportunities policies, perhaps even become a world leader in reducing those unemployment statistics.'

It would be a start, at least.

Serious, with a small frown scrunching her forehead and her eyes thoughtful, she said, 'Why?'

Her neck flushed, as if her own candour had shocked her.

'Why what?'

She took another sip of wine, gave a small shrug. 'I get it. You want your company to have a social conscience.'

His jaw tensed. 'My company *does* have a social conscience.'

'Sorry. That sounded…flippant of me. What I mean is, why does it matter to you so much? I would have thought you're busy enough running Lancaster IT and the charity. What is it that motivates you?'

Wasn't *that* the question? And he understood her curiosity. He longed to peel back *her* layers, to expose her secret yearnings, her belief systems, her philosophies on life. Her reaction to flying had completely thrown him. What had made her so cautious?

'It should be important to all of us.'

At his non-answer, Libby nodded.

Then he completely stunned himself by adding, 'My sister had an intellectual disability.'

His gut twisted, stealing his appetite.

'I wish more people had cared about *her* potential, her future.' Himself especially.

What a time to open this particular can of worms. Why had he brought up his sister? He *never* spoke of Jenny. To *anyone*. Let alone someone he'd just met. What had prompted him to tell this intriguing virtual stranger his motivations? Especially when he barely picked over them himself for fear of what he'd expose.

But, even though their acquaintance was in its infancy, didn't some small part of him already feel closer to her than the hours they'd known each other warranted? She was easy to talk to. She cut through the bullshit. He didn't have to second-guess her every thought and unspoken subtext. And she wasn't constantly flattering him.

Perhaps it was just his dick doing all the thinking. Even so, the most serious of his ex-girlfriends knew nothing about Jenny. Well, nothing *he'd* spoken about. Gossip notwithstanding.

She gave a small nod, her eyes watchful. 'Had?'

It was common knowledge—his professional success and the prominence of his family name had exposed his entire life to public scrutiny. Of course the media had sensationalised the tragedy—the intellectually disabled teenaged daughter of a wealthy family dying from an epileptic seizure had been big news for all of thirty seconds. But they hadn't covered the devastating impact it had had on his parents' marriage, his mother's subsequent nervous breakdown or her intermittent dependence on alcohol.

'She died.'

He swallowed hard, his failure a bitter taste on the back of his tongue.

'I want to offer respite facilities for parents, so they can take a break, recharge, focus on themselves and their relationship. I'm building a purpose-built rural hotel here in the Oxfordshire countryside. Somewhere families can come, where the children can be occupied with the Able-Active programme while the parents get some well-deserved down-time. It's important. Something that gets overlooked.'

Something that could have helped *his* family, perhaps.

She was quiet for so long he was half tempted to fly her back to London, pay her for her time and release her from their deal before she pulled out.

She sipped water, her shrewd eyes flaying him alive.

'So what's on the adrenaline menu tomorrow?'

Thank fuck.

His breath stuttered back to life. 'I'll show you the site of the hotel.'

Her stare held his, bold, astute, daring. 'And…?'

If she kept looking at him like that he'd never make it through one mouthful, let alone a whole meal.

'I thought we'd go hot air ballooning.'

Her composure wobbled, her throat working on a swallow. 'Seriously?'

He nodded. *Quid pro quo, Olivia.* That stunt last night had cost him dearly in the self-denial stakes. Time to return the favour, make her step outside her comfort zone for a good cause, let down that tightly bound hair of hers until her eyes lit up from within.

Her controlled sigh gusted over parted lips, the tip of her tongue darting out. 'Well, that's going to cost you.'

Blood surged to his groin, his limbs twitchy with contained energy. What would that tongue look and feel like on his dick? What would he do to see it there?

'What do you want?' He spoke slowly, his words measured, voice low.

With almost Pavlovian predictability his body responded to the question he'd asked. A question he'd wanted to ask her all day. A question that sounded more like a dare.

For a second her eyelids drooped, her chest rising and falling with shallow breaths that lifted her alluring breasts. Then she composed herself, gave a sexy tilt to her head.

'Well, for starters I'd like a tour of your bedroom.'

He asked her again. 'What do you want, Olivia?'

He was pressed up behind her, his words husking out with his warm breath on the back of her neck.

She practically melted into a puddle on the plush carpet of his palatial master suite. She'd barely registered the opulence and modern elegance of his home as he'd led her here. Every ounce of her focus had been required to keep herself upright and seemingly in control of her own body.

His words—so intoxicating—wrapped themselves around her, a warm cradle. She fought the urge to succumb to them, to blurt out her every wish, every fear, her very soul to him. But she pulled back, forcing herself to stay in command of herself and the heady situation.

If she couldn't have what she wanted, she'd have what she needed right now. And that was Alex.

He'd agreed to play this game by her rules. The fine line of control and concession was a greased tightrope under her feet. But if he intended to push her out of her comfort zone with daredevil pursuits, she'd push back. Force his natural alpha tendencies into submission. See how far she could take him before he snapped.

She turned, and his warmth seared the tips of her breasts mere millimetres from his chest. 'I want you to watch me strip.'

He nodded, face grim, nostrils flared. Euphoria surged inside her, robbing her limbs of structure until she stepped backwards to the bed, pressing her legs against the mattress to keep herself upright.

Just like the night before, Alex stayed where she'd directed him. His limbs twitched as she worked the buttons loose on her blouse, his palms curled into white-knuckled fists.

Libby slid the silk from her shoulders. The slow glide was torturous on her sensitised skin, which prickled under his heated stare until every tiny hair stood on end. She unclasped her bra, releasing aching breasts, and tossed it on top of the blouse.

'*Fuck...*' Alex hissed, eyes almost black, staring blatantly.

Libby felt his gaze slide over her nipples as if he'd touched her with those slightly callused hands of his. Her knees buckled. She could almost *feel* his mouth on her breasts, his bold tongue laving and lashing. In denying him, she denied herself, but the reward would be worth the wait.

She unzipped her skirt with trembling fingers and hooked her thumbs into the waistband, pushing both it and her panties to the floor in one swoop. Every second she tortured him, she tortured herself. The need to see him naked, to touch him, clawed at her, stifling the breath in her lungs until her head buzzed with lack of oxygen.

He teetered towards her, rocking on the balls of his feet.

'Keep the shoes.' Gruff. A command.

Libby raised one brow, a twist to her mouth. 'Is that what you want?'

His command thrilled her. Hers to concede or deny. She'd love to see the excitement flare in his eyes as it had when she'd unclasped her bra. But this was *her* game. *Her* rules.

He nodded, his stare travelling the length of her naked body, stopping to linger on her breasts, the juncture of her thighs and the four-inch heels. When his eyes detoured to the scars on her left hip, she shifted her arm, hiding them from his view. She couldn't go there.

His chest rose and fell, his fingers clenching and unclenching at his sides, and Libby guessed she didn't have long to enjoy the power trip. But it was worth it. Any scrap of command she held over the scorching chemistry between them kept her grounded, reminding her that this was a game. No feelings allowed.

With a small smile she steadied herself on one of the simple posts of his contemporary four-poster bed and removed first one shoe and then another, her challenging glare pinning him to the spot.

The muscles of his jaw bunched as he lost the battle to meet her eyes and flicked his gaze over her nakedness once more.

'What do you want?' His sexy voice held an almost desperate edge.

Libby exhaled. He was still with her. His reactions matching her own.

'I want you naked.'

She'd barely finished speaking before he'd heeled off his shoes and reached behind him to tug his T-shirt up and over his head. He tossed it away, his other hand tugging at the button fly of his jeans, and with rapid jerky movements pushed his jeans and tight cotton boxers down his muscular thighs, kicking them away.

Libby's mouth had forgotten how to make saliva. She'd been right. His body was a magnificent display of long lean muscles encased in golden skin and scattered with a liberal sprinkling of dark hair, and it stole her ability to think. Her eyes followed the dark scatter of hair covering his pecs, touched on the ink decorating one shoulder and one side of his ribs before dipping to the trail of black hair below his navel that merged with the thatch at the base of his spectacular manhood.

Her brain shut down completely. Alex Lancaster, a specimen of male perfection in his prime, was completely at her disposal.

Awareness returned, and the slight chill of the dimly lit room countered the fire raging inside her. Her nipples pebbled, and moisture gathered between her thighs, She pressed them together to ease the hollow ache inside.

He rolled on the balls of his feet, every muscle tense as if he was forcing himself to stay away from her, at the distance she'd set.

'What do you want?'

More desperation, mimicking the same thing firing along every nerve ending in her body.

'I…' *Him*. She wanted him. 'What do *you* want?'

His stare burned into hers. 'Everything.' His voice a low rumble. 'I want all of you.'

As if slapped, she sobered. His stark declaration brought her back to her senses. She couldn't give him that. She'd done that once. Loved. Planned. Built a future. And she'd lost it all.

The floor solidified under her feet and resolve returned. 'I want you to fuck me.' *That's all*.

In two long strides he reached her. His mouth crashed to hers, guided by her tug to the back of his neck, and she moaned, the relief so overwhelming that if he hadn't banded his arms around her waist, she'd have collapsed to the floor. Her fingers tunnelled through the silky strands of his hair and she parted her lips, welcoming the surge of his powerful tongue with one of her own. Her hands roamed, glorying in the smooth fragrance of skin stretched over hard planes of taut muscle, every inch of him a tactile feast for her fingertips.

He slotted one thick thigh between her legs, the spring of his chest hair grazing her nipples as he pressed closer. Libby rubbed her wet sex on his leg, the friction sublime, but not nearly enough. She tore her mouth from his, her head spinning with an oxygen-deprived head-rush.

'Now, Alex. *Now*.'

She reached between them, her hand circling his hard length, the satiny skin sliding over the steel beneath as she worked him from root to tip.

He stared, his chest working furiously, his mouth swollen and his eyes heavy-lidded.

She wanted him inside her. *Yesterday.*

With a grunt, he lifted her, depositing her in the centre of the bed and following her down. But rather than settling himself between her spread thighs, as she craved, he dipped his head to her breast, his mouth covering her nipple, sucking her inside the moist warmth.

Libby cried out, her flash of disappointment banished by sublime pleasure. Better than she'd imagined... the fantasy a poor relation to the reality. His cheeks hollowed as he drew more of her flesh inside, his tongue flicking the nub erect and then his teeth scraping with just a bite of pain—enough to shoot sensation to her core in a prelude to the spasms she hoped would soon follow.

As if he'd seen this arc of sensation he spread her thighs wider with his knees, his fingers finding her slick centre, homing in on her clit with pinpoint accuracy and the perfect amount of pressure.

She whimpered, her fingers frantic in his hair as he abandoned one nipple in favour of the second. There was no reprieve from his relentless barrage. His tongue laved, his fingers swirled and plunged, and Libby forgot to breathe as coils of rapture wrapped around her from the inside out.

His dark lashes fluttered open, his stare finding hers as his mouth curled around her breast.

'Alex...' She was close, so close. She wanted him inside her, but she wouldn't make it.

He growled—a feral noise from the back of his cultured throat, as if encouraging her over the edge. Libby latched on to the dark swirls of his irises as his mouth and fingers continued to drag every drop of bliss from her strung-out body.

Her orgasm blindsided her, slamming her back into the mattress with a ragged cry. The spasms rocked her. Alex kept her thighs spread with his, his hand working furiously and his mouth relentless at her breast.

She shoved at him, the pleasure too intense. But he'd drained her of any strength she possessed and her hands flailed uselessly at his shoulders as he abandoned her clit but continued to suckle at her sensitive nipple.

'Stop…please.' She lay boneless, her head swimming.

He pulled back, releasing her from his wicked mouth and pursing his swollen lips to blow a stream of air over her wet, puckered nipple. He smiled. A predatory kind of smile. If she'd had any energy she'd have clawed back command of the situation. But she could only watch as he crawled over her, his lips grazing a path from her ribs across her belly and to the tops of her thighs.

He held her open, kissing first one thigh and then the other before staring at her sex with uninhibited candour and blowing cool air over her wet lips.

'Alex…' He'd completely disarmed her. And he still hadn't given her what she'd asked for. This was *her* game. *Her* rules.

With a lazy smile he kissed one thigh again and then climbed from the bed. His muscular ass flexed as he strode to the nightstand. Amazed that she had any hormones left, Libby licked her lips. The clench of his buttocks and the jut of his thick, proud cock was enough to create an impressive second wind.

What was happening to her? She should leave. Show him she was still in control here. But she craved him inside her as much as she enjoyed her power over their liaison. Shoving away doubts, and the sting of memories, she focussed on him, compelling her breathing into a deep, regular pattern.

He returned to the bedside, his bold gaze on her as he tore open a condom packet with his teeth and rolled the latex down his length with practised, single-handed skill.

'Come here.'

He held out his hand and Libby moved to the edge of the bed before him. He pushed her back until she rested on her elbows and then leaned over her, cupping her face in both hands and kissing her with a passion that stole her sanity and sent fresh spasms through her pelvis. Pulling back, he splayed his large hands on her thighs, slowly easing her open, his gaze darting between her face and her exposed sex.

The way he looked at her... As if he was seconds away from devouring her whole. And that was exactly how she felt. *Consumed.* His stare alone took her there.

'I'm going to fuck you now. That's what you want?'

She nodded, her blood boiling, any snarky retort lost behind her paralysed tongue. If she'd thought business-man, philanthropic, surfer dude Alex was hot, this de-termined, focussed man scorched the flesh from her bones.

He leaned over her, jaw rigid, and locked his arms

either side of her head. Libby lay back, shifting her hips to the edge of the bed. He looked down between their bodies, his bottom lip caught between his teeth. With one hand he gripped the base of his magnificent cock and angled the tip at her entrance. Slowly his gaze locked with hers, and with the scent of sex wafting up between them, carried on a wave of body heat, he pushed inside her.

'Alex—'

His mouth stole her words, his kiss searing as he stretched her, working his way in to the hilt. She whimpered, her nails raking his flanks and her calves pressed to his glorious backside, encouraging him all the way in.

Pulling back from the kiss, he removed her hands from his back, one by one, and his fingers slotted between hers as he pressed their joined hands into the mattress beside her head. Staring down at her, he began to move. Slowly at first, letting her body grow accustomed to him. But then he clenched his jaw and picked up the pace.

Libby closed her eyes—and then slammed them open again, unwilling to miss one second of seeing him stretched above her, his face contorted with pleasure and beads of sweat gathering at his hairline. This time he'd come. She'd *make* him come.

With every pummelling stroke he shunted her on the bed, the edge of the mattress providing a landing place for the force of his thrusts.

'Libby…' His eyes widened, nostrils flaring.

'What do you want?' she asked.

She saw the battle in him, and knew she'd give him

anything in that moment. Just for the thrill of witnessing his loss of control. The knowledge that *she* took him there.

He released her hands. 'Touch your nipples.'

Another command. But she complied, too delirious to care about power play. Her fingers plucked at her breasts, twisting and rolling. Alex watched, his jaw hardening, and a strangled groan rumbled up from his chest.

His hips jerked in a relentless pounding that pushed her closer and closer. When he reached one hand down between them, pressed his thumb down on her clit, she exploded, every muscle in her body rigid as her internal muscles clung to his pistoning cock.

Alex roared, his head thrown back, neck taut, his hips slamming home one last time.

'Fuck… Libby…'

He ground against her as his breathing slowed, forcing the last ripples of pleasure from her core.

After long, delirious seconds, he dropped a chaste kiss on her mouth.

Reality surged.

Libby winced as he gripped the base of the condom and withdrew, the slide of him over sensitised tissue bordering on pain. Allowing herself one last indulgence, she watched him saunter to the en-suite bathroom, his gait a little unsteady.

Despite the tremors and aftershocks jarring her body, Libby flew from the bed, donning her skirt and blouse and stuffing her damp underwear into her bag. She'd never undone her hair, but it had suffered nonetheless. Tucking the wayward strands back into their braid as best she could, she slipped on her jacket just as a still gloriously naked Alex re-entered the room.

He stalled. 'You're leaving?' His sexy, just-fucked features hardened.

'Yes.' Shoulders back, as if she was convincing herself.

He raked at his dishevelled hair. 'And if I wanted you to stay?'

She swallowed, lifting her chin.

She couldn't stay. She'd wanted a fuck. She'd got what she wanted. It had to be enough.

He understood. His jaw bunched and he looked away with a small nod.

Without another word he tugged on his discarded clothes. The atmosphere in the room that still smelled of the intimacies they'd shared chilled Libby to the bone.

Alex grabbed his keys from the dresser, turning to lance her with his black stare. 'Will you at least stay in my hotel?'

He shoved his free hand in his front pocket.

Her face burned as if craving the slide of his warm palm. She missed the warmth in his amber eyes. Missed his smile.

Libby nodded. She couldn't expect him to fly her back to London—not if they had to return here in the morning to put their lives at the mercy of a wicker basket and a giant nylon balloon.

'I'll drive you over.'

'I can live with that.'

CHAPTER SIX

ALEX RAPPED ON the door of one of the hotel's standard rooms, biting back his frustration. He'd instructed the duty manager to give Olivia the best suite—an elegant penthouse with spectacular rural views of Oxfordshire's rolling countryside—but clearly she'd undermined him.

He'd never met such a stubborn, independent woman. The women in his past had been happy to accept his wealth, take his gifts and his generosity, share his affluent lifestyle.

The door opened and his annoyance evaporated. The sight of her sucker-punched him in his gut. She'd pulled her hair into a high ponytail—he'd yet to see her long hair down, wild around her face—and she wore jeans and a long-sleeved shirt. He'd had her belongings delivered to the hotel from London last night, after she'd begrudgingly accepted his offer of accommodation.

Hadn't that been a kick in the balls? He'd wanted her in his bed. He'd fantasised about releasing her hair from its strict braid, waking to find the glossy mass splayed over his pillow or, better, his chest. He'd hoped to spend the night, or this morning, or both, between her shapely thighs, dragging reckless abandon from her with every orgasm. But she'd denied him again, drawing him back to the bargain they'd struck.

It was still dark outside. In the dim glow of her darkened room behind her, he saw her laptop open on the bed. Had she been working? Speaking to someone in America? Booking a flight home?

'Ready to go?'

He clenched his jaw, teeth creaking. He knew nothing personal about her outside of the fact that she was a vegetarian and hated helicopters. Nothing he hadn't gleaned from her company website and her business profile.

Time to change that.

She nodded, her hair swaying. His palms itched to wind that hair round his hand and draw her close for a good morning kiss. The one he'd have given her if she'd awoken in his bed this morning. The one she'd cheated him out of.

He forced his hands to relax.

She glanced down at his side. He held out the puffer jacket embroidered with the Able-Active logo.

'A gift. It gets pretty cold up there.' He pointed skywards.

She blinked, face stony and a little pale, eyeing the jacket as if it was stuffed with snakes, not duck down.

'Thank you. But gifts aren't necessary.'

So prim this morning. Unlike last night, when she'd twisted his hair so hard she'd almost scalped him.

'No?' *Fuck*, it wasn't as if he'd handed her diamonds, or even flowers. 'But here it is anyway.'

It was just a jacket. He doubted she'd packed any serious outdoor gear for a business trip.

'Is there a problem outside of the gift?'

Perhaps she was as cranky at waking alone as he was. Perhaps, like him, she'd woken fully aroused and feeling around the empty bed, the rush of erotic memories making her groan into her pillow. Perhaps he should abandon the hot air balloon trip, suggest they relocate to the palatial suite he'd reserved for her upstairs and christen every surface until he'd made her come so many times she wouldn't be able to help the smile on her face.

She shrugged her bag onto her shoulder and closed the door behind her, reaching for the jacket. 'I'll borrow the jacket—but only because I didn't plan on any wild adventures when I packed.'

Fuck, that smoky voice of hers reverberated through him—another slug of lust. She marched ahead down the corridor, in an excellent move that gave him full access to the view of her denim-clad curves swaying as she walked.

When they were sitting in his Mercedes S-Class side by side, as he navigated the lanes of the Oxfordshire countryside, he glanced over at her striking profile.

'Nervous?'

She stared out of the window, as if formulating her answer, then sighed. 'Yes.'

Her hand rested in her lap. He gripped the wheel to stop himself reaching for it, uncertain of her mood.

'I've been before. You'll love it. And it's perfectly safe.'

She turned on him, eyes blazing. '*Is* it? How do you know that?'

She really was nervous. Perhaps he should have fed her first. Or organised a punt on the river. But he'd wanted to wow her—give her a trip she'd never forget, one she'd embrace when she planned his charity's marketing. But impressing her, it seemed, was no easy feat. And Able-Active wasn't named Able-Relaxing.

'I'd never let you get hurt, if that's what you're worried about.'

She looked away, her pouty lips pursed. 'You can't guarantee that. People get hurt all the time.'

His need to know more about her personally solidified.

'Have *you* been hurt?'

He recalled the irregular silvery scars he'd spotted on her hip last night. Scars she'd tried to hide. He'd interpreted her reaction to the helicopter as first-time nerves. Assumed her caution was just a personality trait not in keeping with the driven and professional businesswoman. But perhaps there was more to her reticence.

'I—I was in a motorbike accident. Three years ago.'

Her gaze returned to the hedgerows and the fields of gold and green beyond, which reflected the first rays of the sunrise lighting the horizon.

His throat thickened. 'I'm sorry about that.'

He should have asked about the scars, but it had been obvious she didn't want to talk about them, didn't want to talk at all, and he'd been overcome with the sight of her naked and her husky command that he fuck her.

'Were you badly hurt?' His ribs pinched, stalling his breath.

She shook her head, shoulders sagging a little. 'Just some superficial cuts and grazes. I was lucky.'

He breathed again, more determined than ever to get to know her while showing her a good time. But perhaps he shouldn't push this. If she'd had a traumatic experience in the past, the last thing he wanted was to force her to relive it.

He pulled off the road, steering the car down a bumpy lane that opened up to a gravel courtyard and some converted stables. Killing the engine, he turned to face her.

'We're here. Look, we don't have to do this. We can get a feel for things, watch a few balloons go up, meet the owner. He's a friend of mine. If you're worried, we don't have to fly. I don't want to make you uncomfortable.'

But I'd love to put a grin of exhilaration on your beautiful face.

Her dark eyes held him hostage. 'I want to do it.' She looked down to her clasped hands in her lap. 'I... I just...'

Vulnerability poured from her in waves. He ached to hold her. To kiss the frown lines from between her brows. To abandon his plans for the week and hole up with her in his Oxfordshire estate, wining and dining her, peeling back her layers, exploring every facet of her fascinating personality.

He held out his hand, palm up, over the centre console between them.

She glanced down and then back up at him, throat

moving on a swallow. Slowly, as if she thought his palm might be electrified, she placed her hand in his.

His chest expanded, a surge of oxygen energising him as it always did when he brokered a difficult business deal.

'Let's just have a look around. If you want to go up, we can. If you don't, we'll just watch a few balloons take off and then go and meet Jack early.'

She scrunched her brow. 'Jack?'

'My cousin. He's an architect and property developer. He's visiting the hotel building site I want to show you today.'

She nodded, clearly reaching a decision. 'No. I want to go up.'

He grinned. She was so determined. So possessed. Completely hardcore. However much she downplayed her accident, it must have shaken her up. It would shake anyone. And yet she was still willing to buy into his grandiose scheme to show her a good time and his vision for his outdoor adventure charity.

He squeezed her fingers. 'Let's *do* this.'

'It's amazing!' She clung to him.

He wanted to keep her prisoner in this basket for ever. Her arm was snaked around his waist, her hand under his jacket forcing a fist into his chest to massage his heart until the blood sang through his arteries.

He positioned his body behind her, his arms either side of her, holding the lip of the basket in front of them, his chin on her shoulder, seeing what she saw.

'Having fun?'

Her hair tickled his cheek and he pressed a kiss to the soft skin of her neck. *Fuck*, when she bestowed that rare and beatific smile on him, he felt like a king.

She laughed—a throaty sound that shot straight to his balls.

'I wouldn't go *that* far.'

Her heart pounded so hard and fast, he could feel it thrum through his chest where he was pressed against her back.

'I can't believe how beautiful it is up here.' She rested her head back against his shoulder, a small shudder leaving her.

If he'd orchestrated a huge romantic gesture, he couldn't have anticipated a more perfect reaction from her. She softened against him, her body heavy, pressing back, covering him from thigh to shoulder. Every time the burner fired and the balloon lurched gracefully higher she laughed, or caught her breath and pressed closer—as if she trusted him over the sturdy basket and the balloon's skilled operator.

The only way to improve on this morning would have been for them to have woken side by side, slaking his need to constantly taste her, feel her, be inside her.

What the actual fuck was *happening* to him? He barely knew her, but already he wanted more of her.

'Tell me something…' His lips traced her earlobe, catching the small gold earring dangling there. Would she play the game they'd started over dinner last night? Would her personal admissions soften like her body?

She sighed—a soft escape of air. 'I'm a trained yoga instructor, although I haven't taught for many years.'

He groaned, his imagination running wild. 'Fuck, could you *be* any hotter? I don't suppose there's any chance of a naked demonstration of the Downward-facing Dog?'

'Pervert!'

Her chuckle warmed his blood, lifting him higher than the balloon could ever carry him.

'You tell *me* something.'

Her words echoed his and he grinned. She relaxed deeper into his chest. Her delicious scent tickled his nose.

He took a deep breath. 'I was a game developer in my teens. A real bona fide computer nerd.'

And he'd had the dodgy haircut to prove it—a detail she *didn't* need to know.

'I guessed. The T-shirt yesterday kinda gave you away.'

He loved it that she was so observant—that she *saw* him.

They watched the horizon in strangely comfortable silence, with only the birds for company. He'd just pointed out the spires of Oxford in the distance when his phone vibrated in his pocket.

His stomach dropped. He'd given Molly strict in-structions to forward all calls but one to Jeremy in his absence. That meant he couldn't ignore this call—no matter how rude it seemed to answer, or how badly timed.

He stepped back enough to fish the device from his pocket, keeping one arm banded around Libby's waist.

'Mother.'

A pause. Acid surged into the back of his throat.

'Zander? Is that you?'

Hairs prickled on his neck. He knew that wobble in her voice. Dreaded it. Eight in the morning and she'd likely drunk so much she couldn't remember who she was calling. Or she'd suffered one of her 'spells', during which she could barely function, shutting herself away for days on end.

'Where's Clive?'

His mother's second husband protected Alex from the worst of his mother's issues—something he was grateful for and felt guilty about in equal measure.

'Golf. I just wanted to say I'll see you Saturday, at the wedding…' Her voice trailed off but the line stayed connected.

Fuck.

'Mother? Maman?'

He'd have to go to her. What if she'd drunk herself into a coma? What if she'd taken something?

Firing a text to Clive, he swore under his breath.

Releasing Libby, he turned and spoke to the pilot.

'Is something wrong?'

Libby touched his arm, dragging him back to the present, away from a past that refused to lessen its hold on him no matter what he did.

'I need to visit my mother. She's…unwell.'

Still grieving for Jenny, all these years later. Reminding them of their loss with her bouts of depression and her periods of drinking too much. Fanning the flames of his guilt for his own shortcomings.

He could have been a better brother. A better son. It

might not have saved Jenny—he wasn't to blame for her death after all—but it might have made all their lives a little easier. Salvaged his parents' marriage. Made Jenny's short life happier.

The balloon began its descent, taking the atmosphere with it. Libby paled, as if her own fears, her own demons, had resurfaced with his ill-timed family interruption.

'It's not serious.' He gripped her cold fingers. 'I just need to make sure she's okay, wait with her until her husband gets home.'

Or organise another stay at the rehab facility where his mother practically had her own room, she'd been there so many times.

Libby nodded, her fingers squeezing his in a display of affection that seemed to shock them both. He gripped them, reluctant to let go of the tenuous trust they'd established.

'I'll arrange a car to take you back to the hotel.'

He'd have to cancel seeing Jack, and Libby's tour of his state-of-the-art respite complex.

His spirits plummeted to the ground with the soft landing of the balloon, his thoughts traversing well-worn pathways of self-doubt. Would he *ever* be good enough to compensate for Jenny's death?

Libby pulled the black velvet ring box from her purse and wrapped her fingers around it, enjoying the familiar comfort of it filling her palm. She still carried it everywhere, even after three years. She didn't need to open the lid. The contents—an exquisite princess-cut diamond solitaire—were a symbol of her life before the motorbike accident that had killed her fiancé a week before their wedding.

The ring itself, whilst precious, represented a happier time of her life. A carefree time when she'd believed anything was possible and life with Callum had stretched before her in an adventure akin to those Alex planned for his clients. The adventures he insisted on showing her.

Libby placed the box back inside her bag without opening it. Normally she stared at the ring's beauty as if it were a talisman to ward off the image of Callum dying in her arms on the hard, unforgiving asphalt. When she thought of him, the ring helped her to remember him alive and vibrant, with excitement lighting his eyes as he'd proposed. But today her handsome fiancé's face was a little harder to recall, his image blurry, as if photographed out of focus.

She pulled out her phone, firing a text to Alex. She barely knew him outside the physical intimacies they'd shared and their brief working relationship. But the defeated slump to his shoulders as he'd walked away earlier had stirred something in her. Feelings she'd thought long-ago abolished. Dangerous feelings that teetered too close to the edge of caring.

Hope your mother is okay. Thanks for the ride today. I can see why Able-Active clients will love it.

She opened her laptop, picking up on the work she'd begun last night and continued that morning when sleep had had no use for her.

On the surface, the marketing strategy for Able-Active presented little challenge for Libby. Secure corporate sponsorship, launch a national campaign to publicise the charity to a clearly targeted audience and streamline the charity's website and social media presence with an online sign-up form.

But Alex's passion for the work had spilled over, infecting her. It meant so much to him on a personal level. She wanted to do the best job she could. Make it the success he hoped for.

Her phone buzzed. Alex.

Thank you. She's fine. I'm sorry I had to rush out on you.

His answer left her strangely hollow. The ache that had begun when he'd been buried deep inside her last night intensified. The game of getting-to-know-you they'd started was frustratingly incomplete. Game-playing with Alex fed something in her she hadn't known was starving.

Her fingers hovered above the screen of her phone, desire and denial warring for control.

What do you want?

She was playing with fire. But the flames flushed her body with energy. *Irresistible.* Her days here were limited. How much harm could one week do? And she could be called home at any second, their time together cut short, if Sonya's baby decided to put in an early appearance.

He took several minutes before his reply, as if the answer wouldn't come. Minutes in which Libby was certain she'd lost him. That he no longer wanted to play.

I don't want to see you. I don't want to undo your hair and wrap it around my hand. I don't want to make you come. What do you want?

His reply brought a smile to her lips. He'd fully embraced the rules, turning them against her. Clever man.

With trembling fingers and clenched thighs, Libby fired a response that had her breathing fast.

I want you to stay away.

She dropped the phone and rushed to the en-suite bathroom. She had no idea where he was or how long it would take him to get here. But she knew he'd come.

She took a quick shower, taking extra care to fasten her hair securely into a severe French pleat, no strand left free. It seemed he had a penchant for her hair. His hints and requests were glimpses into his desire to see it wild and free, which only intensified her need to push him until he couldn't help but undo her hard work.

She slipped on fresh underwear and her favourite comfortable jeans and sweater. She'd barely had time to slick some gloss onto her lips and wave a mascara wand over her lashes before there was a knock at the door.

He'd aged. Wearing the same charcoal-grey T-shirt

and jeans he'd worn that morning, he slouched in her doorway, one muscular arm braced on the doorframe. His intense stare was hooded, his mouth tight, and whilst his hunger electrified the air that separated them, something was different. *He* was different.

She opened the door wider, inviting him in and battling the urge to hold him until the lines around his eyes disappeared. But she couldn't step that close to the edge. This was all she could offer...all she could accept. This game—short-lived, finite and slaking only a mutual physical need.

The door closed behind him and he followed her into the room.

She turned, begging him with her eyes not to break the spell, not to break the rules. 'What do you want?' she said, her voice a whisper.

He stared. Endless seconds in which she felt stripped bare by the intensity in his haunted eyes.

'I want to be buried inside you.'

Stark, honest, hard to deny. But deny she must. For her own sanity.

Without comment, or even acknowledgment, she stripped out of her sweater and jeans, careful not to disrupt her hair. His eyes widened at the lacy underwear she'd donned, but he stood stock-still, waiting and watching.

She approached him as a cat might approach a dog: with slinking bravado, narrowed eyes and muscles coiled tight, ready to flee if he decided to show off his superior strength.

When she was inches away she sank down, catching

him by surprise. Her knees hit the carpet at his feet. She unclasped his belt buckle and made quick work of the button fly of his jeans. When she lifted her eyes to his smouldering stare she caught her breath. How had she ever thought she could control this vibrant, fearless, worldly man?

Every muscle in his body seemed to strain, and raw power poured from his dark eyes and clenched jaw. His biceps bulged at the sleeves of his T-shirt as he fisted his hands at his sides.

Uncertain how much time she'd have, she tugged the jeans and underwear down over his hips, her mouth watering at the sight and scent of him.

Leaning forward, she touched her tongue to his steely tip.

'Wait.'

Her gaze flicked up. Would he stop her? Had she imagined the excitement flashing in his dark eyes? Perhaps his brooding mood had left him reluctant to play her game. Obey her rules.

Slowly his hands cradled her face, fingers burrowing into her hair. She pressed her lips together as one by one he tugged the hairgrips free, until her hair spilled down her bare back. He stroked it back from her face, gentle hands fingering the strands with a reverence that made her itch.

Libby looked away. She didn't want to see tenderness on his face. Didn't want to explore his strange mood or the reasons for it. She just wanted *him*. In her mouth, at her mercy, under her control.

She gripped his erection, angling him towards her

mouth, and closed her lips around him. He groaned, his teeth snagging his bottom lip. His thighs were steel under her palms and he shifted restlessly on the balls of his feet, his chest rising and falling in rapid pants.

Boldly staring up at him, she took him to the back of her throat, her tongue pressed hard against him to hit all his pleasure points...the ones that made his eyes roll back and his hands fist in her hair. But his stare quickly returned to the action, darting between her eyes and her working mouth while harsh grunts jerked from his panting chest.

'Libby...'

When he tried to back away Libby clung tighter, increasing the suction, her head bobbing with renewed determination. Power surged inside her, flooding her sex with moisture. This big, strong man—intelligent, driven, compassionate—was trembling, frantic, on the verge of shattering. And, although he was legendary for his thrill-seeking and audacious business deals, he'd handed her control like a precious gift. A gift she needed.

With a shout he came, his hands buried in her hair, holding her face as she sucked and swallowed until he was spent and breathless, a wondrous expression softening the hard planes of his face, which seconds before had been twisted in rapture.

She released him from her mouth and he hauled her to her feet, engulfing her in his strong arms and then gripping her face to kiss her with heat.

He pulled back, leaving Libby's head spinning.

'Never go back to America.'

Not bothering to wait for her response, he kissed her again, looped his arms around her waist and flopped them down onto the nearby mattress.

CHAPTER SEVEN

LIBBY'S HEAD ROSE and sank with the movement of Alex's chest as his breaths slowed. His warm fingers traced small circles on her back, his legs entwined with hers, and his heartbeat thumped under her cheek, which was glued to his sweat-damp skin.

It was way too intimate, but her heavy limbs refused to move—as if they'd run a marathon and gone on strike. And in a way they had. This week was a whirlwind of life in the fast lane so far.

'I'm sorry I had to leave so suddenly today.'

His sleepy voice rumbled in his broad chest, his chest hairs tickling her nose.

'I understand. Is your mother okay?'

He drew in a breath that seemed unending, the gust of his prolonged exhalation blowing strands of her now wild hair onto her face. His fingers swooped in, pushing the hair back from her forehead and rectifying the situation.

'She drinks sometimes. Too much. She's never really got over losing Jenny.'

The weight of his confession pressed Libby even further into the mattress and her breath stalled. Should she pry? He wouldn't have mentioned it if he didn't want to talk, right?

'What happened to your sister?' She held her breath.

His fingers returned to the small of her back, their tips gliding round and round in a hypnotic pattern. 'She had epilepsy.'

Libby waited, still and quiet, so as not to break the confessional spell.

'Around six hundred people per year die of sudden unexpected death in epilepsy. It's called SUDEP for short.' His fingers on her back stilled. 'She was eighteen.'

His matter of fact tone contrasted with the increase in his breathing and the renewed thud of his heart.

'I'm sorry that happened to your family. It must have been a terrible time.'

'For my parents, yes. It essentially destroyed their marriage. The blame game. The what ifs. Although theirs had been a rocky marriage for years prior to my sister's death.'

His hand resumed its stroking.

'Do you like weddings?'

The change of subject was so abrupt Libby lifted her head to stare at him, her neck muscles jarring. What could she say? He'd opened up to her this evening—not that it was part of their deal—but she wasn't ready to do the same. What was the point? This was temporary. A holiday away from reality. Less than a fling—a business merger, brokered and negotiated. Just sex.

She trained her features to stay neutral, swallowing back the acid in her throat. 'Who doesn't?'

She shifted, untangling herself from his warmth and his long, muscular limbs. She sat on the bed with her back to him, reaching for a robe and shrugging it on. A shield.

'Do you want to go to one? My cousin Isabel is marrying in France this weekend. We should have met her brother, Jack, today. The architect I told you about.'

Libby swallowed. That itchy, impatient feeling was back, making her restless. 'You can't invite a stranger to a family wedding.'

'Why not?'

His fingers continued to work their magic, circling lazily on the curve of her hip. Even through the cotton his touch carried a potency that made her weak.

'You'd be my plus one. Jack and Isabel's grandfather owns a château near Nice. Ever been to the south of France?'

'No. But that's not the point.'

His hand slipped under the robe, locating the lace of her panties at her hip. The glide of his fingertips distracted her racing mind.

'Is it that you don't like my chopper?'

Her lips twitched. The sight of him, relaxed, playful, a self-satisfied grin on his decadent mouth as he sprawled naked on her bed, soaked the panties he was now burrowing inside.

She needed to change the subject. *Fast.*

She forced her features into a stern glare. 'What's on the adrenaline agenda for tomorrow?'

His grin widened, as if he sensed her diversion tactics. 'Jet boating. On the Thames. I need to be back in London.'

His probing fingertips traced the crease of her groin, his knuckles brushing the crotch of her panties.

She rolled her eyes, biting her lip to contain the swell of excitement.

'I have plenty of work to catch up on too. My latest client is super-demanding.'

Why didn't she just push his hand away? Kick him out of her hotel room?

'He is?'

He pressed down on her clit through the damp fabric, stilling her breath. His voice dropped an octave. Was that a hum of satisfaction? At finding her wet?

'I thought he was super-accommodating.'

Her gaze flicked down his ripped chest and abdomen to the thickening cock on his thigh.

'If you want to scrap the thrill-seeking we could *both* get some work done.'

Cool speech had become increasingly difficult, and the words emerged slow and sluggish.

He grinned, one fingertip circling. 'But the adrenaline is the best part. And what about our deal?'

Libby spread her thighs a fraction. She needed more. Wanted more. Mention of the deal had returned her equilibrium. No more talk of weddings.

He sprang up from his slouch, gripping her waist and expertly tumbling her under him. Air slammed from her. His face, an inch above hers, had lost its playfulness.

'Come jet boating tomorrow.'

His thighs slotted between her legs, spreading her open. His teeth caught his bottom lip and he pressed his erection to the damp lace separating them.

Her robe had fallen open. His fingers curved under her bra straps, tugging them over her shoulders as his mouth trailed kisses over the tops of her breasts.

His argument was persuasive. She breathed out an, 'Okay...'

He tugged one bra cup lower, exposing a nipple to his voracious mouth, and then he lifted his head, eyes wicked. 'Good. Because I was about to ask you what you want.'

Although his wandering mouth made speech difficult, she told him—and he complied.

Something tickled Libby's shoulder, her thigh, the back of her neck... Groggy, she stirred aching limbs.

Warm, minty breath brushed her earlobe.

'Wake up, beautiful. It's time to fly.'

Alex.

She cracked open one eye to find her hotel room in darkness. 'Time is it?' She flipped onto her back to see him dressed, his hair damp, presumably from the shower.

'Early. My chopper awaits.'

He pressed a chaste kiss to her mouth, his lips soft and languorous. Despite his chiding, his eyes were playful.

She groaned, her arms looping around his neck and pulling him down. 'Come back to bed.'

He chuckled into her neck. 'I'd love to. But adventure calls.'

His hand slipped under the covers again, fingers sliding up her thigh and zeroing in on her clit so her eyes popped open and she squeezed her thighs together, trapping his hand.

'Thanks for not kicking me out, by the way.'

His lips brushed her ear, her neck, and the sexy rumble of his voice thrummed through her nipples in time with his exploring fingertips.

'My creeping-around-like-a-teenager days are over. Skulking out of my own hotel at three in the morning would have been highly embarrassing.'

She sobered.

She *should* have kicked him out. Shouldn't have invited him back to bed. Snuggling, sleeping together, waking up to his mouth on her—*not* part of the deal.

Batting away his hand, she shot out of bed. 'Do I have time for a shower?'

She ignored his slightly bewildered expression, which heated as it travelled over her naked form. 'Yes. But if you don't want company in there I suggest you hurry. I had hoped to wake you up with my mouth between your legs, but I took pity on you. You were out of it.'

Libby swallowed. Both images—her drooling in her sleep and him waking her with his spectacular oral skills—sent her heart fluttering behind her ribs.

She dived into the bathroom, flicking on the shower and jumping in before he could make good on his word or before she relented and surrendered.

She almost jumped through the glass cubicle when he said, 'So, about this wedding…'

He lounged in the doorway, and Libby was grateful for the frosted glass.

'Do you mind? Some privacy, please.' She poured shampoo into her hair, glaring at his smirking face.

His gaze took one last, lazy tour. 'I've touched most of your body with my tongue, inside and out, and now you want *privacy*?'

'Yes.'

Infuriating man. Bathroom-sharing was definitely *not* part of their relationship.

He shrugged and moved just behind the door, so he could no longer see her but she could still see his reflection in the bathroom mirror.

He raised his voice over the sound of the spray. 'I don't usually have to beg for dates. You're crushing my ego.'

Now he'd mentioned the 'D' word she definitely couldn't go. Even though she'd never been to France. It was on her wish list. Not that she took holidays any more.

'Go away.'

He laughed. 'Aside from the journey there, I promise no daredevil stuff.'

'Weddings are for families.'

Damn, she'd already used that argument.

'I told my mother about you and she thinks you should come too.'

Shampoo ran into her eyes and she winced. 'You told your *mother* about me?'

'Yes.'

'Why?' Without the non-verbal cues, it was difficult to know what he was thinking.

'She needed cheering up. Her second husband is American. She'd *love* to meet you.'

Libby stepped from the shower, shutting off the water and wrapping herself in a fluffy, white towel.

'I'll think about it.'

Her heart wasn't in this argument. She blamed the remnants of jet lag and last night's lack of sleep. But she had no intention of going to his cousin's wedding or meeting his family.

She fastened the towel around her chest and stuck her head through the doorway.

'Aren't you too tired to fly?'

There was no way she'd get in that contraption again if he felt under par.

His gaze gave her the once over. 'Nope. I'm good.'

'Because, strictly speaking, a helicopter ride and jet boating counts as *two* activities.'

He stepped closer, eyes predatory. 'Will it cost me?' His hands found her hips, fingers clenching in the thick towel that scraped her sensitive skin.

She leaned closer, her lips tingling to taste him. 'Yes...' A whisper. This close to him she could barely think, let alone negotiate.

His eyes gleamed. 'I look forward to it.'

He smacked a quick kiss on her lips, leaving her reeling, and headed for the door.

'You have ten minutes to dress that sexy body of yours.'

With a cocky wink, he was gone.

* * *

One hour and one hair-raising helicopter trip later, Libby found herself back at Waterloo, on the banks of the Thames, squished into a life jacket. She'd assumed he had a jet boat and that it would be a private ride. He did, of course, own a jet boat—but he'd booked them into a tourist ride. Apparently this added to the 'fun'.

Alex squeezed her hand. 'You okay?'

She nodded, incapable of voicing any of the tart replies queued up on her tongue. Why put herself through this? Why didn't she tell him to stuff his high-profile account up his gloriously muscular behind?

Trouble was, now she'd experienced his sexual prowess the stakes were higher than the deal being simply good for business. And, despite her reservations, the exhilaration and serenity of the balloon ride had been an experience she'd never forget.

He smiled—half-mocking, half-indulgent—and scooped her close with his arm around her rigid shoulders. His lips grazed the top of her head, her forehead, her temple.

'You're perfectly safe. This skipper is the most experienced. Wait until you see their reactions.' He tilted his head in the direction of the other participants, lined up on the dock. 'Feel the sheer thrill of it yourself. I want to make this affordable and accessible for my kids. They'll love it.'

Libby looked at him. Saw him clearly as if for the first time. Excitement glinted in his eyes, transforming their colour from dark chocolate to amber, and his hair

lifted in the wind, giving him a boyish air, incongru-
ous with the powerful, urbane man she knew him to be.

And he practically vibrated with energy. He'd called
them 'my kids'. This venture fed his soul.

A pang of jealousy rolled in Libby's stomach. It had
been a long time since anything had fed her own with-
ered soul. A strict diet of hard work and trigger avoid-
ance had left her seriously malnourished in recent years.
She'd pushed aside her own passions, blocking out anything that made her remember Callum, the life she'd
planned with him, happier times…

Her reverie came to a halt as she followed Alex to
the front of the sleek powerboat. He'd commanded the
best seats in the house. The ones with a direct view of
the ride ahead and in line with the inevitable faceful of
Thames river spray.

Libby pressed frigid lips together. 'You owe me big-
time for this,' she muttered as she took her seat, her
hands gripping the icy handrail in front.

He laughed, tugging her closer to whisper, 'Why
doesn't that feel like *any* kind of hardship at all?'

Before she could formulate a tart reply, the engine
fired up and they were off.

It had been a long time since she'd had so much fun.

The boat bumped along, taking her stomach for the
ride, and she had a unique view from her vantage point
of the iconic landmarks lining the Thames. The infectious screams and laughter of those sharing the journey
added to the excitement as he'd predicted. Alex gripped
her hand tightly, his face full of laughter every time the
boat lurched and she screamed.

By the time she was safely back on dry land she already craved a repeat performance.

Alex kissed her, their wet cheeks sliding, cold lips clinging around their mutual grins. 'Told you.'

'You were right. Must suck, being you.'

He sobered, unclipping the straps on her life jacket and then removing his own.

'Sadly, I have some work to do this afternoon.' He brushed a wet lock of hair from her face, his palm warm and dry against her hot skin. 'I need to play the boss for a few hours.'

His scorching stare told her he'd rather do all the erotic things currently running through her dirty mind, but then he seemed to take command of himself.

She nodded. 'I could work.'

She had stacks to do. For him…for her other accounts. Why did that admission carry less reward than it had a week ago? She *lived* for work. This job in particular would be incredibly lucrative in professional kudos. Why was playing hooky with the charming, contradictory CEO so much fun?

He took her hand, turning them away from the dock. 'Work it is. I'd like you to put together a short presentation, if that's okay—of the ethos behind Able-Active.'

She nodded, her mind racing with ideas.

'I think I've given you enough of a taste to know what we're about.'

'Okay.'

'And, if you're free, I'm hosting a gathering for possible benefactors and investors tomorrow evening. Hopefully my speech and your presentation will help them part with some cash.'

As she followed Alex to the sleek car waiting for them the thrill of sitting at her desk, even working on such a worthwhile project, carried far less weight than it should.

A very worrying turn of events.

CHAPTER EIGHT

THE MARIE ANTOINETTE suite at the Ritz brimmed with elegantly dressed bodies and suited waiting staff. The gilded Louis XVI–style décor and sparkling chandeliers bounced light around the crowded room, which hummed with the chatter of multiple conversations and the tinkle of fine crystal champagne glasses.

Libby focussed on the heat of Alex's hand in the small of her back, which was burning through the simple black silk shift dress she'd packed for any social function that arose while she travelled. Not that it was flashy enough for these surroundings, but she was here to do a job—not parade the latest couture.

Alex had already told her she looked beautiful, despite the simplicity of her outfit. Once in the doorway of her hotel room, when he'd pressed her up against the wall and kissed the freshly applied lip-gloss from her mouth, and again when he'd dug his fingertips into her hip as they'd left his car, whispering to her how he looked forward to repaying his debt for their trip on the river earlier this morning.

Libby shivered. Nerves? But the assembled guests,

hand-picked by Alex as possible investors and benefactors to Able-Active, presented a small and hopefully
captive audience. Could her jitters have something to
do with the way he kept his hand on her at all times?
Circulating the room with her, introducing her to too
many people to remember, his act of possession as un-
nerving as it was thrilling.

'Thank you, James. You're doing a great job.' Alex
addressed one of the waiters and took two glasses of
champagne from the young man's tray.

Libby accepted a glass, noticing that James made no
eye contact and rushed away more quickly than perhaps
he should have.

'The waiting staff are all kids from the Able-Active
programme,' Alex murmured. 'James has autism.'

Libby nodded and glanced around the room. These
young, smartly dressed waiters and waitresses weren't,
she guessed, typical for the Ritz.

Molly arrived by their side. 'They're ready when you
are, Mr Lancaster.'

Alex nodded and handed his PA his glass of champagne. Turning to Libby, he brushed her temple with
his and whispered, 'Wish me luck.'

Before she could reply, he made his way to the front
of the crowd, where a small podium had been set up.

Libby watched, heat pooling in her belly, as he took
his place behind the microphone and commanded the
room to silence, his demeanour relaxed and engaging.
He didn't need luck. His determination and enthusiasm
alone could win over the entire room. No wonder he was
so successful. His passion and drive were infectious.

'Ladies and gentlemen—friends.' The dazzle of his confident smile traversed the crowd, landing here and there in recognition and greeting. 'Thank you all for coming tonight to the launch party for Able-Active. Many of you—business associates, mates from uni, partners in crime—know me well.'

His genuine smile made an appearance. Not the reserved, polite one that lent him an air of authority, but the wider, unrestrained version that deepened the grooved dimple in his cheek and showed his playful side.

Libby felt her belly flutter, remembering that smile trained on her this morning in the jet boat.

'You know what this charity means to me, but most of you don't know why.' He indicated a framed photo of a teenage girl on the dais beside him. 'If Jenny, my sister, was alive, she'd be thirty-five years old now.'

The room fell deathly silent. Libby's pulse thrummed in her throat.

Alex sobered, his chin dipping and his voice deepening to a reflective rumble. 'I often wonder what kind of adult life she'd have had. Would she have fallen in love? What kind of job would she have enjoyed?' A pause, his eyes scanning every member of the audience. 'Did she dream of being a mother? Have aspirations to help others, or want to run the London Marathon?'

Alex glanced again at the photograph, his eyes dimming.

'I was fifteen when eighteen-year-old Jenny died. I don't recall her goals, her passions, her ambitions, aside from the fact that she wanted what the rest of us have. Opportunity, choice, equality.'

He touched the edge of the frame holding his sister's image.

'Jenny's short life was good. She laughed a lot, she smiled all the time and she loved to dance.'

He gave a small smile—intimate, as if he were alone in the room.

'But it could have been better. The only employment opportunity open to her when she left school was a few hours a week volunteer work. She required help and support to do many of the things other teenagers take for granted, and many things, due to lack of trained carers or simply lack of facilities, weren't an option for her and others like her.'

His throat worked, Adam's apple bobbing.

'I could have been a better brother.'

A long silent pause filled the room with skin-crawling discomfort.

'I want a better future for teens like Jenny, and with your help, your support, Able-Active will be a starting block towards a level playing field and opportunities for all. Thank you.'

Libby's gaze, glued to Alex, travelled the room with him as he became swallowed up into the crowd, accepting handshakes and back-slaps. He'd mesmerised her—mesmerised everyone in the room, no doubt—with his heartfelt and humbling speech.

She wanted to find him. To kiss him just because her mouth missed his and she couldn't think of a single reason not to. But Molly touched her arm, reminding her of her own presentation.

She dragged her eyes away from Alex, handsome in his dark suit, smiling and working the room with practised skill.

Molly spoke first. 'Ladies and gentlemen. Can we please have a round of applause for the waiting staff this evening, who are all participants on the Able-Active programme and have been trained by the staff here at The Ritz?'

Libby's palms stung as she joined the applause, her cheeks aching with the depth of her smile.

'And now I present Libby Noble, from the New York firm Noble and Pullman, to tell us a little more about Able-Active and Mr Lancaster's vision for the future.'

Libby swallowed, flicking the remote to begin her presentation, which would be projected onto the screen behind her. Following Alex's speech was going to be daunting, and she had no hope of matching the impact he'd had on the room. Her goal was to add to it, to complement the picture he'd painted with her own impressions, throwing in a sprinkling of marketing jargon and creating a buzz among the assembled potential supporters.

She glanced down at her notes, stomach churning. The careful, measured words she'd prepared were dancing on the page, as if mocking her with their caution and their detachment.

She cleared her throat. 'Able-Active isn't a unique charity.'

A photo of kids enjoying a kayaking trip that Libby had lifted from the website appeared on the screen.

'Worthwhile? Yes. Rewarding? Yes. Essential? Yes. But what is *exceptional* is the vision, passion and motivation of Alex Lancaster as their CEO.'

The image changed to a photo Libby had taken of herself on the hot air balloon. Her smile shone from her eyes, against a backdrop of the rolling green of Oxfordshire and the distant views of the city spires.

'This is more than outward bound. This is real life opportunity. The chance for meaningful training, employment and recreation for vulnerable members of society who often get overlooked, pigeonholed as having nothing to contribute.'

The picture changed again to a shot of their trip power boating on the Thames. Libby's eyes were scrunched closed as a blast of water sprayed her and Alex in the face, and Alex's delighted grin was firmly on her.

Lifting her eyes, she homed in on his watchful stare across the room. She folded her notes in half, her throat tight but her chest expanding with words that came from her heart, not her head.

'I came to London to work, with recreation the furthest thing from my mind. It's been many years since I participated in anything that carried an element of risk or provided that slam of adrenaline.'

Her insides quivered, her breath stolen by his continued intense focus. The same focus he offered in the bedroom.

'But I haven't felt more alive, or had so much fun since I myself was a teenager.'

She looked away from him, feeling the slow boil of desire now circulating where her blood should be.

'I'm certain that we all know someone who would relish the current Able-Active recreation experiences as much as I have enjoyed sampling some of them this week. And I'm sure we all know someone who would love the chance to have a proper job—one they can take pride in. There are many families who need support—a break from caring for their loved ones with extra needs. Able-Active, with your support, hopes to meet all those challenges. Thank you.'

She moved from the podium to a round of applause, her legs shaky. Molly guided her towards Alex, whose stare still devoured her from across the room.

Halfway there, she found her progress interrupted by Jeremy Wells.

'Great speech.'

He snagged a flute of champagne from a passing waitress, his dismissive and slightly aggressive move surprising the girl so that her whole tray of drinks wobbled.

Libby hadn't liked Jeremy the first time they'd met. She liked him even less now as he derailed the fledgling waitress's carefully woven path through the partygoers.

Libby accepted a glass and thanked the girl. Reluctantly she turned her attention back to Alex's financial director. His suit, whilst clearly expensive, erred on the too-small side, and his paunch obscured the waistband of his trousers and stretched the buttons on his shirt to bursting point.

Tingles—the bad kind—snaked up Libby's spine.

'I'm sure the funds will come rolling in now.' His eyes gleamed, dipping to Libby's chest.

Creep.

'I hope so.' The hairs on the back of her neck prickled to attention. She didn't want to appear rude to one of Alex's valued employees, but this guy made her skin crawl.

Her gaze sought Alex and escape. Sadly he too had been intercepted and was deep in conversation.

Libby stepped aside, making her intention to escape clear.

Jeremy touched her arm, his fingers quickly dropping away at her frosty glare. 'So, I'd love to show you the sights before you leave London. Are you free tomorrow evening?'

He stepped closer, eyes flicking south again. Clearly he had the hide of an elephant—or was simply ignoring her subtle *fuck off* vibe.

Libby fought the urge to cover her cleavage with her hand. 'I'd have loved to explore London—' *just not with you* '—but every second of my week is committed to my work for Able-Active.'

She stretched her lips into an insincere smile.

'Excuse me.'

She weaved through the bodies, coming to a halt at Alex's side. With their backs to the opulent room's ornate fireplace, he rested his hand at the base of Libby's spine, fingers splayed. She breathed out a sigh.

'Olivia, I'd like you to meet Jack Demont—my cousin, and brother of the bride at this weekend's festivities.'

The handsome Frenchman dropped a kiss to the back of Libby's hand. 'Delighted to meet you, Ms Noble.'

Like Alex, he was tall, his striking eyes partially obscured by a flop of dark blond hair.

'Please, call me Libby. Your English is excellent.'

Unlike her French.

Jack laughed. 'Thank you. My father is English and I spend a lot of time here. Plus, I had my accent bullied out of me at school by some notorious thugs.'

He flicked a glare at Alex, who laughed and shrugged, unapologetically.

'You gave as good as you got.' He grinned a lazy smile at Libby. 'I wore braces for much of my schooling.'

So Mr Perfection had once had flaws? A computer geek with braces? She shivered, certain that her fifteen-year-old self—an insecure bookworm dressed from the thrift store—would have found him attractive.

Alex turned back to his cousin. 'I've invited Libby to Henri and Isabel's wedding.'

Jack bowed his head in acknowledgment. 'Yes. You must come. Provence is stunning at this time of year.'

'I'm sure…' Olivia looked away.

'I don't think Olivia is big on romance,' said Alex.

Libby shot him a look she hoped conveyed her contempt. Why would he assume that? He knew nothing about her because she liked it that way.

The sting of his jibe called her a liar. Didn't *some*

part of her relish that they were getting to know each other? Not that she'd consciously let him in. She never let *anyone* in. But with his confessions about his mother and sister, his open, raw vulnerability—he'd lured her dangerously close.

Jack slid wary eyes between her and Alex, seeming to sense the tension sparking in the air. 'Well, excuse me. I'm leaving for Nice tonight.' He kissed both of Libby's cheeks. 'It was delightful to meet you. I hope you'll accept my cousin's invitation to the wedding so we can get to know each other better. *Au revoir.*'

Jack departed, talking the room's warmth with him.

Goosebumps raced along Libby's bare arms. She turned to Alex, the take-down she'd planned dying on her lips at his proximity.

He pressed close, leaving the scantest space between his body and hers. 'What did Jeremy say to upset you?'

His breath gusted over her neck, her shoulder, spreading tingles.

She met his hard stare, felt the flickers of heat melting her insides. Was that jealousy? Possession?

'How do you know I'm upset?'

His perusal completed a tour of her face, lazily tracing each feature in turn. 'I've seen you happy, relaxed, excited, replete…' He mouthed each word, his lips and tongue caressing her, as when he'd drawn those emotions from her. 'I'm observant where you're concerned.'

His fingers found the sensitive skin inside her elbow, sliding. The intimacy, for once, was irritating.

She bit her cheek. She shouldn't have let Jeremy get to her. She'd met enough Jeremys professionally to be able to handle them. And, unlike Alex, they were easily forgettable and easy to walk away from.

Libby shuddered, the imprint of Jeremy's fingers still tainting her arm, and his greedy stare still burning her skin.

'Did he come on to you?' A flash turned his eyes molten, burning into hers.

Why lie? She owed Jeremy nothing. And this thing with Alex was temporary. No time for insecurities.

'Yes.'

But didn't she feel his possession in every touch? Crave the spark of it in every look he gave her? What was wrong with her?

His fingers stalled on her arm, the press of the tips a fraction firmer. 'Are you interested?'

'What?'

Eyes hard, he thinned his lips. 'Well, we're just fucking—*your* word.'

Libby glanced around to see if anyone was paying them any attention. She had given this thing a crude label, one that clearly outlined the parameters of their contact. Why, then, did hearing her words turned back on her irk so much?

Alex continued, as if unconcerned, but his voice was low. 'I've asked you on a date. A proper date. No games. You haven't answered.'

So he did have an ego—better hidden than most, but there just the same.

'I don't sleep around.' Why tell him that? It made no difference to them. They barely knew each other. Their fuck-fest had a short expiry date. 'Before you, there'd been no one for three years.'

He didn't register her confession. She wasn't even sure why she'd told him herself.

'So why me?'

She lifted her chin, backpedalling. 'Fishing?'

He sighed, his gaze flicking away and then returning, more open. 'Yes.'

At last there was a hint of insecurity in the way he rubbed the knuckles of one hand down his face.

Tempted to tease him, Libby pinched her lips together, hiding a smile. She grasped the chance to lighten the mood, steer them away from the wrong turn this conversation had taken. After all, they weren't a couple, so why bother with disagreements? Their time was limited.

'Temporary lapse of common sense.' She smiled. 'I blame jet lag.'

After a couple of beats he grinned, his hand slipping to her waist and his expensive, heady scent filling her head as he dipped closer.

'Want to be reckless with me tomorrow?' His lips grazed her ear. 'Jet skiing?' He whispered the words as if he'd suggested an illicit sex game.

She shuddered. The thought was not unpleasant. 'Another day freezing on the Thames?'

His mouth twisted, dimples flashing. 'No, I was thinking the Med…' His cocky disarming smile returned.

Irresistible.

'Like to get your own way, don't you?' Her breath

gusted, her pulse fluttering in her throat. Any game with Alex was surprisingly addictive.

'Absolutely.' A slow nod.

Clearly sensing victory, he moved closer, his hand sliding to her hip. Seductive.

'And so do you.'

He quirked an eyebrow, fingers gripping tighter, the way they did just before he came, as if he couldn't get close enough, deep enough.

Lust sizzled between her thighs.

This had to stop. She needed to start weaning herself off this exhilarating ride. She wasn't his. Couldn't be— no matter how right her hand felt against his slightly callused palm.

Time to rein back some control over herself. 'And what do you want right now?'

Hooded eyes held hers. 'I want you to go back to your hotel tonight.' His voice dropped. 'I want you to stay in London tomorrow while I fly to the South of France.' His lips touched her ear, whisper-soft, starting a chain reaction of fine tremors. 'I want you to keep your panties on under that dress so I can't go down on you in the back of my car.'

Libby's knees buckled and she wobbled on her heels.

Bastard. He knew the effect he had on her.

Pulling away, he twitched his decadent lips. 'But, ladies first. What do *you* want, Olivia?'

He'd become so good at her game. *Too* good. But why did breaking the rules with him feel better than getting her own way? And wasn't she still getting what she wanted?

Him.

Still, she tried to discipline herself and her spiralling feelings. 'I'm tired. I want an early night.'

His face fell.

'I'll meet you in the foyer in five minutes if you wouldn't mind giving me a ride.'

She spun on her heel, ignoring the flash of uncertainty in his eyes.

When she emerged from the ladies' room, her panties tucked inside her clutch bag, and rounded the corner to the main hotel foyer, Alex was waiting for her, hands stuffed in the pockets of his pants, an intense, heated stare following her progress.

She couldn't resist. She loved holding him on the brink, disarming him as much as he disarmed her. Redressing the balance so that when she walked away she'd have no regrets.

She made it outside with the minimum of wobble, every step, every second she kept him dangling increasing the throb between her legs.

Alex's driver opened the door of the sleek limo and Libby ducked inside, Alex's hand on her arm, guiding her.

Once inside, the driver said, 'Where to, sir?'

From his seat opposite her Alex raised a questioning brow, a hint of challenge and a large slice of vulnerability in his eyes. How had she missed that before? It was *her* call—as always with him. Aside from pressing the wedding date, he'd always extended her the ultimate control. It was the main reason she was still here. Should she give in one more time? Or should she ration her encounters with him, wean herself from her addiction. He'd never know about the panties.

She licked dry lips. 'Where do you stay when you're in London?' Her throat was scratchy.

Eyes dark, he watched her from the seat opposite. The air crackled with tension, electricity arcing between them when not even their knees brushed. Libby regretted the spaciousness of the luxury vehicle. Right now she'd give anything to be sandwiched next to him in the back of one of those charming Mini Coopers.

He shrugged. 'I have a place in Belgravia.'

Of course he did. She nodded, holding his bold stare with one of her own.

'Eaton Square, please, Roger,' he said.

The car rolled into motion, entering the central London stream of traffic, as constant as the flow in New York.

Alex raised the privacy screen between them and the driver with the touch of a button.

His gaze pinned her. Hot, defiant, demanding.

'Show me.'

The bite of command entranced her—hers to obey or deny. Fire raged inside her, hot enough to melt her clothes away. Placing her clutch on the leather seat with a shaky hand, Libby slowly lifted her dress, millimetre by millimetre, so the fabric bunched at the top of her thighs.

'Wider.' His nostrils flared and he spread his own thighs, as if seeking comfort for the confined bulge at his crotch.

She loved to push him. To see him teeter on the brink of that glorious moment when he shucked his impeccable buttoned-up manners and proper English upbringing and dived for her, eyes glazed with lust.

'Bossy, much?' She pressed her thighs together. This was *her* game.

He nodded. 'I want to give you what you want. What *I* want.' His tongue touched his bottom lip. 'Let me.'

Yes.

With a sigh she couldn't contain, Libby conceded. Her legs parted, knees spread wide, her heels digging into the luxury carpet. She met his stare, bold, daring, counting the seconds until he snapped.

With a curse, Alex dropped to his knees, his hands gripping her thighs and spreading her open wider to his brazen look.

'Do you understand what you do to me?' His eyes sought hers in the car's gloom, his gruff voice pricking her nerve endings alive. It was a whisper. 'Do you feel the power you wield? Power over *me*?'

Libby stopped breathing. His questions were as close to any true emotions as they'd ever expressed, and they struck close to her own, so close her skin seemed to tighten and shrink.

She gripped the leather beneath her palms to stop herself from pushing him away and jumping from the moving vehicle.

What had started as a game—a risqué diversion of give and take—now erred perilously close to a chasm of emotion she daren't cross.

Sex. This could only be about sex.

She focussed on breathing, her inhalations matching the tempo of his while they waited, watched, warred.

Alex broke first, a sigh gusting from him. 'I can't do this any more.'

Libby's stomach flipped. 'Do what?'

The rumble of the car's engine faded away as the world stuttered to a halt. She only had days left with him. She wasn't ready for this to be over—wasn't ready to think about the end of this wild, hedonistic ride.

With the candour she'd grown to expect from him, he said, 'I want you too much.'

His hand skittered along her inner thigh, his eyes seeking her permission before his fingers probed her entrance, which was slick, ready for him. His thumb circled her clit and her head dropped back, her thighs trembling with the effort of staying open to his avid stare.

He leaned over her, his gravelly voice sin-dipped. 'Come with me.'

She was about to.

'To France.'

The fog cleared and she opened her eyes to his penetrating gaze.

'No games, Olivia.'

His fingers continued their lazy swirling, fogging her mind.

'No jet-skiing. No work.'

He pumped his fingers faster.

'Just two people attracted to each other, enjoying a social gathering in a stunning part of the world.'

Libby fought to make sense of his words while her body sang under his hand. He made it sound so simple. And on the surface, it was. But his idyllic scenario was pitted with potholes—landmines of repressed emotion that threatened to blow her carefully constructed and life-saving control apart.

'I…'

He grunted, perhaps interpreting the denial on her face or hearing her unspoken refusal. He shifted, lowering his head between her thighs, his lips kissing her intimately and his tongue flattening against her primed clit.

All thoughts, all arguments fled. Only Alex remained, and the pleasure he wreaked expanded to fill her mind with every swirl of his tongue and plunge of his fingers.

'Yes!' she cried out, her hands tangling in his hair, holding him close as she rocked into his mouth.

The sublime glide of his tongue ceased, and the pleasure drained away to a slow simmer.

'Yes, you'll come to France?'

He kept her on the edge, with his thumb where his mouth had been. Not what she wanted, but enough to prolong the haze.

'Yes…yes…' She'd argue later, rescind her acceptance. Any agreement made under sexual duress was null and void.

'Yes, you'll come…on my face?'

The wicked glimmer in his eyes stole the last of her breath and all she could offer was a feeble nod.

When his mouth covered her again a second finger pushed inside her to join the first. She exploded, her thighs gripping his head and her fingers twisting in his hair as she clung on for dear life in the moving vehicle.

The spasms trailed away and she pushed at his shoulders, breaking the divine contact and missing it at the same time. Before her body had in any way recovered from the intense orgasm she pounced on him, kissing his wet mouth and tugging his belt free. He helped, their fingers working simultaneously to free him from his dress pants. She gripped him, her hand fisting his hard length, her tongue tasting him, tasting herself.

He produced a condom from his pocket and Libby jerked him up onto the seat beside her, snatching it from him in her haste to have him inside her. She covered him, feeling that ache back between her thighs. She didn't want to think about games, or weddings, or the past. She craved him more than ever, more than the first time, her need only intensifying with each time they were together like this.

'Hurry.'

She hitched her dress higher, straddling his lap. One hand gripped the leather upholstery behind his shoulder as the other delved between them to align him at her entrance. And then she was sinking onto him, their mutual groans resounding through the confined space, with only the darkened night outside to hear them.

Alex gripped her face in his palms, demanding eye contact as she rocked on his lap. 'Mean it, Libby. Say you want to stop playing.'

He was pushing the boundaries, changing the game plan. But in that moment she'd promise him anything.

She gripped the lapels of his expensive, exquisitely tailored tux, crushing the fabric in her palms.

Part of her *did* want to stop playing. Part of her was desperate to get to know real Alex, the man, flaws and all. Part of her wished she could be the old, unguarded version of herself. But she couldn't give him everything he wanted…everything she longed to give.

Another compromise? She could shore up her dread for one day. Go to this stupid wedding. Act, smile, drink champagne. Just one day. An end to this fairy-tale week that she hadn't planned for but was powerless to stop.

She tensed her internal muscles, forcing another groan from him. Dipping her head to his shoulder, she traced her mouth in a path along the soft skin of the side of his neck, and feathered his ear with her lips.

'I'll come to France. No games.'

And then she'd head home. Try to forget Alex Lancaster and her European adventure.

His hands cupped her buttocks, taking control of the friction with thrusts from beneath. Libby held on tight, knowing this ride, this time, meant something more, that the stakes had been raised to levels she couldn't afford.

They came together—him with a shout the driver probably heard, and her with the collar of his tux clamped between her teeth. Anything else and she'd have blurted out something suspiciously like feelings. Feelings she had no room for—especially not where a man like Alex Lancaster was concerned.

CHAPTER NINE

LIBBY STARTED AWAKE. The unfamiliar room came into focus and she felt the weight of Alex's arm on her waist, the heat of his naked chest at her back. The dream that had woken her, vaguely familiar in the way recurring dreams were, was still pounding the blood around her body. Always the same. She was searching for something she had no hope of finding, only to jerk awake with the feeling that she'd failed some momentous task and would never be happy again.

She lay still, closing her eyes and slowing her breathing, mindfully scanning her body, willing her tense muscles to relax in the hope of returning to sleep. But, like many nights before, tonight was to be one of mind-racing exhaustion, and after ten minutes she gave up, carefully slid from underneath the slumbering Alex and shuffled to the edge of his enormous bed.

Like the one at his Oxfordshire estate, this bed was a sleek, modern four-poster. He lay sprawled in the middle, his muscular back revealed by the sheets pooled at his waist and his hair a dishevelled mop partly obscuring his handsome, relaxed face.

The tattoo that snaked around one side of his chest was partly visible—a line of script: *Rise by lifting others.* She'd read it fully earlier in the shower, her fingers tracing the ink.

After the limo they'd showered together, soaping and nibbling every inch of each other's bodies until they'd drawn a third orgasm from each other and then collapsed into Alex's very comfortable, too-big bed. Not that he'd let her keep her distance. And Libby had been too tired to object when he'd dragged her by the waist into his spooning.

Finding his dress shirt discarded on a chair, she slipped it on and crept from the room. Her clutch was where she'd dropped it on the hall table. She located her phone and headed for the state-of-the-art kitchen, hoping to find a kettle amongst the seamless cupboards and contemporary appliances.

Within a few minutes she'd brewed tea and was snuggled on an oversized couch, pulling a throw over her legs to ward off the middle-of-the-night chill. A quick calculation of the time difference proved favourable and she dialled Sonya's number. She'd neglected her pregnant friend, sending only daily e-mails. She needed to hear her voice. Reset her equilibrium.

Sonya answered on the second ring. 'What are you doing up? Isn't it the middle of the night over there?'

'Hi, to you too. I couldn't sleep.' Libby sipped her tea, spotting a well-placed mirrored coaster on the minimalist slab that paraded as a coffee table.

'Still jet-lagged?'

Libby longed to pick apart her insomnia with Sonya,

to bounce her unsettled emotions off her friend. She winced. But Sonya was nine months pregnant and solely in charge of their business.

'I guess… How are *you*? I rang to make sure you aren't working too hard.' Libby's throat burned, and she felt inexplicable emotion close to the surface at the sound of her friend's voice.

A long sigh. 'I'm fine. Fit to burst, but fine. I've worked from home these last two days,' said Sonya. 'Vinnie has rescheduled some of my out-of-town appointments for you when you get back next week. Sorry. I guess it's finally catching up with me.'

Libby worried at a cuticle, her shoulders tense. 'Of course. That's absolutely fine. I can come home earlier if you need me.'

She could drop everything and be back in New York in ten hours. No wedding. No more adrenaline. No more Alex.

She barely managed a swallow.

'No need. It's almost the weekend. No one needs you *that* urgently.'

A smile tugged her cheeks. Sonya sounded like her old self. Perhaps she needed *them*. Her friends, her business, her life. That was who she was.

The rush of homesickness tightened her chest, but she suspected the vice would be crossing the Atlantic with her when she returned to New York. The only thing to warm Libby's bed there was Dumbledore, and he hogged the pillow, purred in her ear and had fishy breath.

She scrubbed at her face. Perhaps the idea of a wedding had unsettled her more than she admitted.

'Look, Libbs, I was going to wait until you were back, but I want to give you as much notice as possible. I'm not coming back.'

The silent pause raised the hairs on Libby's arms.

'What? When?'

Libby's tired mind played catch-up.

'After the baby's born.'

'Of course you aren't!'

She should never have left Sonya alone at a time like this. Her friend's voice held a strain.

'No. I mean I want to stay home with the baby. I'm not coming back after my maternity leave. I know it means leaving you in the lurch, but I want to sell my share of the company.'

Libby reeled. 'I understand. Of course you want to be there for your tiny human.'

But I'll miss you.

Tears threatened, closer than ever to the surface. She swallowed them down, hating the selfishness that had enabled her to leave her heavily pregnant friend in the first place, and now bemoaned her decision to be a stay-at-home mom.

Sonya rushed on. 'I won't pull out straight away. I'll give you a chance to find someone you can work with. There's no rush.'

'Don't be silly. I'll be fine. You just focus on you and the baby. I'll miss you, though.' The last words were choked out past a constricted throat.

She wasn't fooling anyone—least of all her best friend.

'Libbs, I'm sorry. I just don't want to feel pressured to return to work, or to feel obligated.

'I understand.'

Did she? She'd spent long career-focussed years trying to forget Callum's death and her own misery. Cheated, she'd closed down that aspect of her life, denied herself sex, relationships, even friendships in case they wandered from the friend zone into something too close to what she'd once had with her fiancé. What she couldn't risk feeling again. But could she call it happiness? Living?

Libby clutched her stomach, holding in the emotion that threatened to send her running for Heathrow Airport. What would she do without Sonya? Her dry sense of humour and her shared passion for cute shoes? They were a team. The *best* team. But her friend was moving on...her life was transitioning to the next phase...whereas Libby had purposely withdrawn from the well-travelled path.

Things shifted, became distorted as if being viewed through a cracked mirror. The wedding, her dream— all so trivial.

'Libbs? Are you okay?'

She pressed the heel of her hand to her throbbing eye socket. 'Yes. Just a bit surprised.' She forced the wobble from her voice. 'And missing you, I guess.'

'I miss you too. Look, I'll help you find a new partner, if that's what you want,' said Sonya. 'I've even mocked up an ad. I'll e-mail it through for you to take a look.'

'Don't worry about any of that now. You just concentrate on resting.'

A sigh she was powerless to stop stuttered from Libby. This was real. The end of an era. The end of the only good thing Libby had left in her life.

But Sonya didn't need any extra burden. Libby forced joviality into her voice. 'I found the cutest little outfit for the baby—just wait till you see it.'

She needed to hang up before the floodgates opened and she sobbed down the phone, begging Sonya to stay.

Sonya's relief brightened her tone. 'Send me a picture. So, what's the sexy Englishman got planned for you for the rest of the week?'

Libby spoke without thinking, her mind still fogged with sadness. 'I'm going to France.'

Sonya's gasp brought Libby back to the present. '*Ooh, la-la. So* not fair. I'm a whale, stuck here with the dreadful humidity, and *you'll* be swanning around Paris.'

A feeble laugh. 'Hardly.'

Pressure built behind Libby's eyes. She scrunched them closed, breathing through her nose. She could no longer hide her true emotions from her friend.

'He's invited me to a wedding.' Her throat shrank, hot and achy, and her voice dropped to a whisper. 'I don't think I can go, Son…'

'Oh, Libbs.' She gave a small sigh. 'Have you told him why?'

'No.' It was too personal for a business associate. And that was the label she felt comfortable with. But weren't they more than that? Their relationship was blurring around the edges… He'd said no more games…

'Well, you don't have to go—come home.'

Home. But without seeing Sonya every day, would her New York life even *feel* like home?

'Look, I know you don't want to hear it, but it's time to focus on *you*,' said Sonya. 'Callum would want you to be happy.'

Libby nodded, although she knew Sonya couldn't see. Her silence spoke of understanding without the need for words.

What *was* happy? And where did she search for it? It had been so long since she'd considered the possibility she'd convinced herself that this—her job, her cat, her friends—were all she'd ever need. But life changed. She knew that better than anyone. Her best friend was moving on. They'd still be there for each other, but it wouldn't be the same. She was truly happy for Sonya. But how could *she* stay the same when everything was shifting under her feet?

'You're right. I just don't know how to do it.'

'Libbs… Don't overthink it. Go to France, drink champagne.' She gave a bitter laugh. 'Have a glass for me.'

Libby sniffed, smiling despite herself. 'Okay.'

'Will you be okay?' Sonya's voice dripped with concern.

Libby injected her tone with a lightness she didn't feel. 'I'll be fine. Thanks for being there.'

'Always.'

'Promise me you'll rest?'

'I will. Promise me you'll try to do what I said?'

'I will. Love you.'

They ended the call.

Libby sat staring at the twinkling lights of the city, her forgotten tea now as cold and unwelcoming as her tumble of thoughts.

Libby opened heavy eyelids, the splash of cold water on her foot startling her from a sun-warmed slumber. Alex stood at the foot of her sun lounger, rivulets of water caressing his tanned, muscular body, which was covered only in a pair of black swim shorts, their wet fabric clinging to his thighs and the bulge of his crotch.

Libby licked dry lips. He was Adonis. Standing on the terrace of this fairy-tale eighteenth-century French château, complete with turrets, he looked as if he'd come from a movie set—or the pages of one of Vinnie's beloved magazines.

She smiled. Her outlandish assistant would pop something if he could see her now.

'Come in. It's warm.'

Libby curled her toes, checking the reality beneath her feet. The whole day had held a surreal quality. A private jet ride from London to the south of France, a waiting car to drive them to this breathtaking château, a delicious brunch on the terrace where she'd met Isabel and Henri, the bride and groom, and now Alex—wet, practically naked—luring her to the pristine blue waters of the estate's swimming pool.

She took his outstretched hand, allowing herself to be pulled from her lounger and into his now familiar embrace. His wet body slid against hers, raising goosebumps, his searing kiss turning her from warm and sun-kissed to hot and achy.

The château, owned by Jack and Isabel's maternal grandfather, had fourteen bedrooms, half of which were occupied by the wedding party. Alex and Libby had sole occupancy of the sumptuous guest wing. She toyed with the notion of dragging him back there now, but perhaps a dip in the pool would cool both her body temperature *and* her libido.

Libby pulled back from the kiss, walked to the edge of the pool and executed a perfect dive into the deep end. When she surfaced Alex was watching her from the side of the pool before diving in himself and surfacing at her side. His arms circled her waist as they trod water together.

'Told you it was good.'

He manoeuvred her to the side of the pool, holding her captive against the tiles while he finished the kiss, stealing her air and plunging her back into tantalising fantasy.

No.

Not again.

She couldn't risk her feelings. The pain wasn't worth the gamble. Fortunately Alex lived on a different continent. Once she arrived back in New York, settled back into her safe, predictable life, these unsettled emotions would fade like her tan. Although without Sonya by her side life would be a little less predictable.

She forced her mind to think about something else. Anything else. But with Alex's lips on her throat and his erection pressed into her thigh beneath the waterline it took every scrap of her resolve.

He provided the distraction. 'Tell me something about yourself.'

His fingers traced patterns at her waist. She almost wished she'd worn a one-piece instead of a bikini.

Libby held his stare, focussing on the amber flecks in his irises until her own eyes burned, infected by the heat spreading from her throat.

Tired of her own games, and the exhausting jumble of her feelings, she blurted out her first thought. 'I grew up in New Jersey, just me and my mom.'

He lifted his chin, encouraging.

'All this…' she glanced around the opulence of the château's manicured gardens and pristine pool '…is completely alien to me.'

His smile dropped and he pressed his mouth to hers.

She twisted away from the sublime slide of his lips, irritation buzzing beneath her skin. 'I don't need your pity. I've made good for myself.'

His eyes hardened. 'I don't pity you.' Another kiss, harder than the last. 'I *admire* you.'

Warmth spread through her limbs. She didn't need his praise, but it was nice all the same. They kissed again. Libby was uncertain who'd initiated it. It didn't matter. The effect was the same—her mind grew fuzzy, her limbs liquefied and she curled her legs around his hips, deepening their kiss and pressing him between her legs, where she wanted him.

Would she even care if someone saw them? With the warm sun on her back and a wet Alex to explore?

He pulled back, eyes hooded. 'I want to see you again—beyond this week.' He pressed her against the side of the pool, as if he guessed his admission would make her want to flee.

She unlocked her crossed ankles, sliding down his body. 'I...'

An image slammed into her mind, as clear as the crystal blue waters of the Mediterranean—Alex, more dates like this, more adventures, a shared life... Her breath caught, her mind flicking a switch to close down the slug of yearning.

She pushed at his shoulders, trying and failing to create some distance. 'I live in New York.'

He didn't give an inch, his body a wall of solid warmth before her.

'So? My mother is French, my father English.'

He spoke with that sultry drawl, tempting her, as if her reasoning had no effect on his argument, as if the benefits were obvious.

He nuzzled her neck again, his lips seductive. 'You forget I have a plane. New York's not that far away.'

For a second her head lolled back as Alex's kiss found the sensitive skin just beneath her ear. Ignoring the flood of heat to her erogenous zones, she focussed on the prickle under her skin.

'Alex... This is just temporary. Just fucking, remember?' She cringed, the words she'd uttered scalding her vocal cords.

His lips ceased their meandering. Libby wished she'd kept her mouth shut as prickles of unease doused the pleasurable heat.

He leaned away to glare at her, their bodies separating an inch and allowing a rush of cool water between them.

'And if I want more?' Eyes hard, the jut of his chin determined—this was the formidable businessman others saw. The driven man used to making things happen just the way he wanted them.

She shook her head. She couldn't give him more. Sometimes you didn't get what you wanted. Sometimes it was snatched away, no matter how hard you clung.

He clenched his jaw, eyes searing. 'What do you want, Olivia?'

For once she had no answer to the now familiar question that had become a mantra for them—a prelude to their game. Wanting him sexually? Easy. Discovering inconsequential facts about his life? Fun. But more than that…?

She considered herself incapable of more. And not with a man like Alex—wealthy enough to pursue dangerous pastimes, driven to recklessness through never having to accept that something was off-limits, an adrenaline junkie who grasped life with both hands…

Not exactly like Callum, but close enough to amplify the chills set off by this turn in the conversation and the increasing physical distance between them.

Had the moment arrived? Was it time to give it to him straight? She'd always been honest with him.

'I want to do a good job for you. I hope I've done that.'

'You have.'

He sensed the brush-off. That was evident in the minute muscle twitching in his clenched jaw.

Libby covered his mouth with her fingers. She couldn't leave him with any doubt.

'I need to get home, to sort out my business.'

Coward.

'Sonya wants out of the company so she can be at home with her baby. I need to find someone to replace her—work out if I can afford to buy her out or if I'll need a new partner.'

New shivers came, and the taste of acid, an ache under her ribs.

He shrank against her thigh, easing his body completely away from hers. Her fingers flexed, desperate to pull him back. But she couldn't lead him on. Couldn't let him think there was any future for them beyond this week, no matter how tantalising the prospect.

'That's all I can think about right now.' All she'd allow herself to think about. 'I'm sorry.' She pressed a brief kiss on his mouth, swallowing back a knot of emotion. 'This has been fun. An adventure I didn't expect. Thank you.'

His eyes narrowed, determination sparking in their depths. 'So let me be clear. You're ending this? You have no interest in seeing me beyond this weekend?'

Yes.

No.

I can't.

Alex's phone trilled from the terrace, saving her from answering. She recoiled, shrinking inside. He gave her a hard stare as he moved away, the chill he left behind spreading to the pit of her stomach.

Then he surprised her by returning just as quickly,

clasping her chin in his hand and lifting her face so their eyes aligned.

'I need to get that.' His sigh gusted over her forehead as he pressed a final kiss there. 'But this conversation isn't over.'

Sprinting across the width of the pool, he hauled his body from the water and in two strides reached the table where they'd left their cell phones.

The final look he'd shot her told Libby he meant what he said. Of *course* he wouldn't give in without a fight—he was a cut-throat businessman, used to getting his own way. Something she admired—a massive part of his appeal, despite her little game of power play.

Libby harnessed her restlessness and the dull ache taking residence in her gut, sinking beneath the water and executing a few invigorating lengths of breaststroke. Perhaps the activity would dispel the hollow space where her vital organs should be. Because if her decision was so right, why did unease hound her every stroke?

Why hadn't she kept her mouth shut for once? Glossed over his proposition, laughed it off, sidestepped the debate with the distraction of their pretty constant need to connect physically? No. The sexual game had been fun—a way to control the inferno of their chemistry— but she wouldn't toy with him.

She sank to the bottom of the shallow end, hoping the sun-dappled water would calm her conflicted mind. Why was there even any debate? It shouldn't matter what Alex wanted. If he'd broken the rules, developed feelings, she'd been honest from the start.

Honest with herself?

No.

It was crazy. In a few short days he couldn't be anything more to her than a holiday fling. Clearly Sonya's declaration had upset her equilibrium. Or the sun, the astounding sex and the glamour of Alex's wealthy lifestyle had forced unrealistic fantasies into her head. Back in New York, with real-life issues, she'd find her balance, gain perspective and a firm hold on her emotions. Right?

When she surfaced, her eyes zeroed in on the object of her discord and a sigh escaped her. The itch beneath her skin intensified. He ended his call, striding back towards her with his confident swagger firmly in place. If she'd dented his ego with her less than enthusiastic brush-off, it didn't show.

He reached for her hands, hauling her from the pool when she complied. 'Maman has arrived. Want to say hello?'

No. She wanted to run away, pretend she'd never met him, try to forget the way he made her feel.

'Sure.'

She snagged a towel from the lounger and wrapped it sarong-style around her body. She'd been gifted a reprieve, but the surge of relief failed to materialise.

'Good.'

He reached for his own towel, looping it around his neck and collecting his phone and sunglasses from the table. With his hand clasping hers, he led them back to the pool house.

'And Olivia?' He gripped her around the waist, his

arm a steel band. 'Don't for one second think we won't revisit that discussion.'

His mouth covered hers, demanding, hot, so easy to yield to. He pulled back, leaving Libby craving more.

'I won't bend on this particular negotiation. I want you.'

CHAPTER TEN

'OLIVIA, I'D LIKE to introduce Marie—my mother.'

Alex slipped his hand to the small of Libby's back, as powerless to stop touching her as he was to dragging his eyes from the swathe of red silk that sheathed her sun-kissed body.

She'd left her hair down, just how he liked it. How she *knew* he liked it because he'd revealed as much. His fingertips tingled and his balls tightened. Her hair did things to him. Dark things.

Fuck, *all* of her did things to him.

'Maman, Olivia is from New York. This is her first visit to France.'

Olivia shook hands with his mother, who, being a French native, insisted on kissing both her cheeks in that European way. Libby engaged his mother in talk of the sights of the local area and the history of the château while he indulged in his favourite pastime—observing Olivia.

She was holding something back. He felt it. When he'd said he wanted to see her again her pupils had di-

172 A WEEK TO BE WILD

lated the way they did when he pushed inside her, their gazes locked.

Her hand in his clung, her fingers frequently slipping to entwine between his, squeezing. When she looked at him she flicked her hair over one shoulder, tilting her head to expose the pale column of her neck. Hiding her unconscious reactions from him was as pointless as her affirmation they were *just fucking*.

His ability to read people formed a major part of his success. And he read Olivia like a screen full of computer code. She wanted more too. Now he just had to convince her to admit it to herself.

He stroked the place between her bare shoulder blades, eliciting a thrill of goosebumps he soothed with his thumb. Her careful evasion should have pissed him off. She'd dressed it up for the sake of his ego, but he'd heard the message loud and clear. And yet gut instinct told him her rejection concealed something else.

Part of him didn't blame her for slamming on the brakes. They'd known each other only a matter of days and long-distance relationships were fraught with extra complications. But something visceral had shifted inside him. The thought of never seeing her again after the weekend left his skin crawling with impatience and his fists uncharacteristically punchy. And *damn* if he didn't want every part of her—complete surrender. Her fearlessness and her insecurities. Her sharp mind and her sharper tongue. Her deepest desires and her greatest fears.

His shoulders tensed, impotence like a block of ice in his chest. He'd indulged her. Conceded too much without pushback. Could he make her see? Draw out what she held back until she admitted what he instinctively knew was there?

He knew one thing for sure—one thing he'd promised her at the pool house. He wouldn't stand by and watch her walk away. Not without a fight.

He tuned back in to the conversation.

'…and, of course, if she were alive she'd have loved this family wedding.' Marie clutched her throat, her eyes turning glassy.

Oh, no. Please let that be water in Marie's glass. The last thing he needed was a scene tonight.

'Maman, it's okay.' He touched Marie's arm, hoping to soothe away the demons his cousin's wedding had triggered. At least he'd told Libby about Jenny.

His mother turned on him, her watery stare blazing. '*Is* it, Zander? You never want to talk about her. She was your *sister.*'

Fuck. He'd guessed this weekend might be a flashpoint for Marie's grief—Isabel and Jenny so alike in looks. His eyes scanned the terrace for Clive. He'd need help if he was to survive this family dinner without a full-blown Gallic scene.

'I know that,' he said.

Fuck, must she always remind him of his sibling shortcomings? As if he didn't relive them every time he thought of his sister. He clenched his jaw and flicked apologetic eyes at Libby, whose own stare had narrowed on him.

Marie seemed to gather herself, and his shoulders relaxed.

'Excuse me, my dear. I'm going to find my husband. It was lovely to meet you.'

Marie touched Libby's arm, shot a hurt look in his direction and turned on her heel, all injured elegance.

Fuck, now he'd upset his mother. He'd hunt her out later. He had a proposition for her—a role at Able-Active that would hopefully give her renewed focus.

'Was that really necessary?' said Libby.

Tension twisted his gut. 'My apologies. Even affluent families have their…dramas.'

Perhaps he could have been a little more sensitive, but his mother had seemed determined to air their dirty laundry.

Libby touched his arm, her eyes softening. 'She's just trying to keep Jenny's memory alive, you know.' She stepped closer, her voice dropping. 'In that way you're very similar.'

Were they? He had his mother's colouring, but that was where he considered the similarities ended. And, yes, in his private moments he catalogued his inadequacies as a brother, but he'd dealt with his grief long ago, channelled it into something positive. Giving back in a way to atone.

'Maybe.' *Fuck*, he was trying to lure this woman into a long-distance relationship—not scare her away. 'I'll apologise. I hope to encourage her to work for Able-Active. Perhaps a rewarding position will make things easier for her.'

Her shrewd stare pinned him. 'Yes. And it will give you some common ground—something you can work on together.'

He shrugged, heat blooming in his chest. She cared—about him, about Able-Active, about his mother. No matter how hard she tried to deny it. Why else would she worry over his relationship with Marie?

She leaned closer, her warm fragrant skin buffeting him, softening the blow of her words. 'It's okay, Alex.' Her voice dropped to a low murmur. 'You both miss Jenny. But it wasn't your fault.'

His mouth filled with ash; his muscles tensed. 'I thought we were just fucking? How do you know what I feel?'

How could she see into him so clearly? Into his darkest places? How could she know him so well?

The jibe hit its intended mark and Libby winced. But she recovered quickly, rounded eyes as dark as night peering into his soul.

'I know you feel somehow you let her down. But, Alex, you were a child. Not responsible for your parents' marriage. Not responsible for your sister. I'm certain you were an awesome brother to her.'

Remembering all the times when as a teen he'd ignored his family, how he'd detested the staring of strangers, how he'd abandoned family outings to hang out with his friends, he swallowed acid.

'How can you know that?' *He* didn't.

Her eyes glowed. 'Because you're an awesome man. Honourable, caring, fun. That came from somewhere.' She placed her palm flat on his chest, its warmth branding him through his shirt. 'In here. It wouldn't be there now if it hadn't been there then.'

She touched his neck, the tip of her index finger finding the hollow at the base of his throat.

'I understand. Your mother is hurting. You're hurting. Don't you see? You both feel like you've let the other down. *Stop*. Embrace the time you had with Jenny. Remember her together.'

'You might be right.'

He mashed his lips together. She claimed she didn't want him as anything beyond a fuck buddy. Didn't want to see him any more. But suddenly she was an expert on his pain?

'And what are *you* hiding from, Olivia?' He had eyes too.

Her hands fell from him, a flash of hurt in her eyes.

Libby looked down at her feet, gave a gentle shake of her head. 'I'm sorry. I'm crossing the line.'

No. She was right about him. Spot-on. He'd charged around throwing time and money at Able-Active, trying to make a difference, to make something he could feel proud of. And he didn't want a line where Libby was concerned.

He cupped her hip, drawing her close. 'I think you see me pretty clearly.' His lips brushed her earlobe, but the slug of triumph at the flurry of trembles that skittered down her spine was short-lived. 'But I see *you* too.'

She didn't move, her stare eating into him.

At last she nodded. 'I know what it's like to lose someone.' Her huge dark eyes shone in the lights around the terrace. 'I understand the guilt.'

His fingers curled until he forced them to relax in case he hurt her. 'Want to tell me?'

The barest shrug.

He held in a curse, scanning the now deserted terrace. Their timing sucked. Everyone else had moved inside for dinner.

His hollow stomach lurched, his appetite long gone. 'Are you hungry?'

She shook her head, folding her arms across her chest to grip the opposite bicep. Goosebumps decorated her arms. He reached for his blazer from the back of a chair and draped it across her shoulders.

'Me neither.' He gripped her elbows, drawing her close. His hand moved to brush back her hair, which lifted in the cool evening breeze. 'Let's continue this conversation inside.'

Was this the chink he'd hoped for? Was she letting him closer? Opening up that last guarded part of her? Would she retreat? Push him further away?

She nodded, taking his hand. He clasped her fingers, aware that the pressure bordered on being too tight, but unable to stop himself. They skirted the house, cutting across the rose garden, fragrant in the falling dusk, and entered the guest wing via the French doors that led directly into the living room.

The silence crushed him. Libby pulled her hand from his grasp and moved away to the sofa. He poured them both a glass of brandy, gulping back a mouthful before joining her. The spirit warmed his belly, calming him. She was still there, rolling his stomach with her too-big eyes.

She accepted the drink wordlessly, her face pale.

After several beats, during which they stared across the chasm, he leaned close and kissed her, tasting the liquor on her soft lips. He couldn't *not* kiss her.

'You don't have to tell me.'

He could guess. Pain shored up the last part of her heart, holding it hostage. He pulled back a fraction, his finger twirling a thick coil of her glossy hair.

'But I want to know everything about you. I ache to know. All about you—what makes you tick, what pisses you off, what brings out that dazzling smile of yours.'

She smiled, a dimmer smile than he knew she was capable of, and then sobered.

'I had a fiancé. Callum.'

Boom. A blow to the chest.

Her eyes shone bright; her sad smile was apologetic. 'He was a lot like you—driven, adventurous, fun.'

Saliva dried in his throat.

Her smile widened, as if she were remembering. 'I embraced it. We had good years.'

The brandy turned to bile in his throat, and something dark and vicious twisted inside him. She was still in love with someone else. Some guy. *Callum.*

Libby filled her lungs. He braced himself for the blow. An end to his hopes for them.

'A week before our wedding we...'

She took a gulp of brandy, winced, placed the glass on the table and shrugged off his blazer. Her stare clung to his, as if she were daring herself to speak without the emotion swimming in her eyes.

'He died. A motorbike accident.' The last words appeared in a rush. A verbal ripping off of the bandage.

Alex's brain fought to tease her words from the rage of emotions tumbling inside him. He placed his brandy glass on the table. Alcohol wouldn't help.

'The one you were in?'

She nodded, her gaze fixed on her hands in her lap. 'I escaped with scratches. He died almost instantly.' Dry eyes lifted to his. 'He slid under the wheels of an oncoming truck.'

He gripped her tight, needing to feel her in his arms as much as he wanted to offer comfort. 'Olivia. I'm so sorry.'

She felt so *right* there. His chest ached as if the mouthful of brandy had burned through flesh and bone.

She was still for so long he wondered if she was shedding silent tears, but his shirt under her cheek remained dry and her voice when she spoke was low, but steady.

'I understand how you feel about Jenny. Survivor guilt. Not a day goes by when I don't feel its claws in me. Even three years later.' She lifted her head, spearing him with a sincere, searching stare. 'But it was an accident. One I didn't cause and wasn't responsible for. It could just as easily have been me who died.'

Words shrivelled in his mouth, their sharp edges pricking their way down his throat. How had she seen him so clearly when he'd failed to join all the dots? How could he let her go when for the first time in his life he felt truly connected?

He brushed undemanding lips over hers. 'Tell me

what you want. I'll do anything—take you back to London, fly you home to New York. Tell me.'

She pressed her mouth to his, surprising him with the passion lurking just beneath the surface. Twisting her fingers in his hair, she angled his head until he yielded under her assault, welcoming the touch of her tongue to his with a desire that matched that simmering in him.

She broke away. 'Don't ask anything of me.'

Her breath gusted over him, the chips of amber in her eyes masking her vulnerability.

There it was. Her limit. Her ultimate demand.

He'd never wanted to deny her more.

She gave him no time to acquiesce. She straddled him where he sat, her fingers tunnelling into his hair as she tipped his head back, leaned over him and kissed him with a desperation that begged.

But he was done with games. He'd told her that in London. And he'd meant it. And now she'd shown him the raw, exposed part of her he wouldn't let her retreat. This time he'd control as much as he conceded, show her what he couldn't ask of her, feared telling her in case she skittered out of reach.

She writhed on his lap, pressing her moist heat to his already steely cock. Her whimpers notched up the urgency raging through him—the need to claim her, to convince her they had something worth exploring, something worth fighting for, something beyond a holiday fuck.

But he wouldn't rush this. Wouldn't allow *her* to rush it. Their chemistry, combustive enough to leave them both burnt alive, if harnessed could be ten times as rewarding. And he intended to show her that.

Libby tugged at his shirt, pulling it from his waistband with frantic fingers. He cupped her arse, grinding her onto his erection until she cried out, biting his lip so he tasted blood. *Fuck*, he loved her demanding side. She knew exactly what she wanted and made sure she got it. And he'd make sure he was there to give it to her.

Slipping one hand under her dress, he edged her lace panties aside, finding her soaked. He'd barely touched her. He located her clit, passing a few swipes over the bundle of nerves until she dragged her mouth from his and dropped her head back on a sigh of ecstasy.

He slid his mouth over her exposed neck, finding the sensitive spot beneath her ear and filling his nose with her unique scent as he pushed two fingers inside her and circled her clit with his thumb.

She was close. He could tell by the way her pants stuttered in her throat. Her hips jerked erratically and her eyes, when she opened them and gazed at him, were largely obscured by the dark crescents of her thick lashes. *Beautiful*. What she couldn't give him in words, in declarations, her body gave him in the abandon she couldn't conceal, in the depth of her stare and the way her fingers clung.

His chest ballooned. He was ten feet tall. A king.

He did this to her. *Him*.

Her internal muscles gripped his fingers. His other hand loosened its clutch on her hip and he lifted the swathe of dark silk from her nape, twisting her hair around his wrist and tangling the ends between his fingers. He held her captive, his hand cramping with the pressure of his working fingers between her legs and his fist entwined in her glorious, thick tresses.

His. She was his. Possession burned through him with the thrum of his racing blood.

She glowed. A beautiful woman on the brink of intense sexual pleasure. His balls tightened. His own lust was a dull kick in the gut, but he intended to prolong this night, to wring every ounce of rapture from her so that when she left him she'd be in no doubt as to the depth of his rapidly expanding feelings and hard pushed to deny her own.

She could run, but he'd make damn sure she couldn't hide.

Her decadent lips parted on a strangled gasp. Her eyes widened, barely clinging to his, and her hips stilled.

His stare wide, so as not to miss one second of her orgasm, Alex gripped the back of her neck.

'Olivia.'

Crushing her mouth with his, he captured her broken cries with deep kisses, swallowing each one.

Her pleasure became his pleasure. Her pain of moments ago his pain. Somehow, in a few short days, she'd come to mean more to him than any other woman.

She quietened in his arms, the last judders leaving her replete and languorous. He lifted her, scooping one arm under her legs and the other around her back, and carried her to the bedroom they shared.

He saw nothing but her. Didn't give a fuck about his business, the charity or even his family enjoying a meal somewhere else in the château. All that mattered was Olivia, and his need to show her exactly what she meant to him.

CHAPTER ELEVEN

THE SHEETS WERE cool at her back as Alex laid her gently on the bed. She searched his stare, trying to deny what she saw there. After his honest declaration in the pool, meeting his mother and witnessing the pain mirrored in eyes so much like her son's, all his pieces slotted together. And his instincts about her own demons? Alex peered far too closely into her soul for comfort.

She'd tried to stay impassive, to distance herself. But in the end she'd been helpless against opening herself up to him. She understood guilt, knew first-hand how it burned away at you, slowly, like acid. And she didn't want that for Alex—couldn't bear to see it destroy what was left of his relationship with his mother. He gave so much of himself. To people, to his charity, to *her*.

When she'd probed him about Jenny, told him about Callum, she'd feared she'd push him even further away than her attempt to do so in the pool. But he stood over her now, slowly peeling her from her clothes and then shucking his own until there was little between them except the unspoken.

Her mouth filled with all she longed to say. But it

was pointless. She was leaving and she wouldn't give him false hope. Wouldn't hurt him even when staying silent left her shredded.

He pulled her up on still shaky legs, her intense climax having robbed her of all but the basic functions of breathing and pumping blood around her body. He caressed her. His eyes and large hands touching on every part of her until she trembled anew with adrenaline. Tenderness seeped from his touch, from his stare. She closed her eyes, struggling to witness the raw emotion spilling out of him. Emotion for *her*. Emotion she longed to accept. Longed to reciprocate.

He pummelled her resolve, pulling her so close that she struggled to breathe. He wrapped his arms around her, tangling one hand in her hair and tilting her head back so he could lavish her throat and upper chest with soft, indulgent kisses.

She swayed, the only thing keeping her upright his strong arms banded around her. She'd never survive this—was already perilously close to the final leap of faith.

'Turn around.'

His words whispered over her neck, skittering down her spine. Helpless, she obeyed, her movements slowed by the easy slide of her hair around his wrist and hand. Not tugging. Never bringing pain, but with enough tension that every hair on her head transmitted pleasure to her strung-out nerve endings. She covered his hand, pressing his palm to her head, feeling what he felt.

He kissed her shoulders, lips gliding, his free hand sliding over her hip as he nudged her feet closer to the bed. Libby's head swam. She scrunched her eyes tightly closed. It was enough to hear the husky command in his voice and to feel the reverence of his touch.

His erection lodged between the cheeks of her ass, the warm, hard length of him shooting tingles up her spine to join with the ones from her stimulated scalp.

'*Fuck*, you're a beautiful woman.' His words tickled her neck, and the brush of his lips at her earlobe buckled her knees.

One hand slid the length of her thigh, gripping behind her knee and encouraging her to climb onto the bed on all fours.

A thrill of excitement fluttered in her belly. She turned her head, her bold stare meeting his over her shoulder. But his eyes skittered away, tracing her back, her hips, and returning.

'Your hair is beautiful.' He twisted his wrist, the thick coil of hair sliding through his fingers only to be captured again. 'I've wanted to do this since the moment I met you.'

His wrist was rolling. Again and again. Her hair tumbling away, then being recaptured. All the while his other hand traced a path of fire from her breast to her hip and returned via her arched back.

Moisture pooled between her legs. Anticipation coiled deep inside. Would he push inside her like this? She felt a bead of moisture in the small of her back, where his hard length rested. This position—the view of her perched on all fours, her hair wrapped in his fist, ready for him, brought the breath gusting from him as sure as her own shallow pants.

She closed her eyes, envisaging him behind her, taking her hard, her hair in his hand, while he grunted out the pleasure he was too far gone to contain. She wanted him wild. Wanted him too impassioned to maintain his gentleman's persona. Wanted him possessive and selfish in his need for her.

'Do you have *any* idea what you do to me, Libby?'

The path of his hand paused at her shoulder, one finger tracing a featherlike trail down the bumps of her spine while he ground the length of his erection into her wet sex. It wasn't enough. She wanted him filling her. Pushing her to the edge again while he shouted her name.

'Alex...'

'I've never wanted anything more.'

His voice was a gruff whisper. He pulled his hips back and she groaned, missing the contact.

'And I can't have you.'

His finger slid between the cheeks of her ass, passing slowly, gliding south.

'Not all of you.'

He found her entrance, fingers probing, a tug on her hair.

'Trouble is...'

His wet finger travelled north again, pleasure dancing under the firm pressure of the tip.

'I want all of you.'

He plunged two fingers inside her, spreading them to open her sensitive walls.

'More than fucking.'

He tugged her hair, tilting her head back.

'More than a few stolen days.'

She twisted, opening her eyes to glance back at him.

His eyes burned with an intensity she'd yet to witness.

'I want it all.'

He latched his stare to hers. The raw hunger she saw in his features, slack with lust, need burning in the depths of his eyes, stole her breath. She had no time to answer or to acknowledge his words. No time to untangle the knotted threads of her own feelings.

Alex released her hair, flipped her onto her back and climbed above her.

His kisses started with her mouth, all too soon departing for her throat and her shoulders. Her restless hands clawed at him, her nails likely leaving marks, but she was helpless, and for the first time in years she was accepting the state instead of trying to outrun it. Completely at his mercy and—for now—*his*.

His mouth lavished her breasts, nipping and sucking until her legs twisted around his in an attempt to bring them closer together.

When he traced her belly with his lips, his hands pushing her thighs apart, she thought she'd die, so great was the need coiled inside her. She cradled his face while he suckled her sex, his grunts of pleasure vibrating through her clit.

His mouth left her abruptly and he kneeled between her thighs, his stare tracing her from top to toe.

'I want all of you. I want you to be mine.'

He reached for the condom he'd tossed on the bed

earlier and ripped into it, his eyes holding her captive, bold, daring her as he sheathed himself.

And then he was pushing inside her, and her hands were clasped in his, their fingers interlocked as if they'd never let go, his stare eating her alive and his body rigid above her like a man on the edge.

His head dipped to her breast once more, his hot mouth drawing out her cries and whimpers as his hips ground into hers. Within two or three thrusts she came, clinging to him with everything she had as the slow-rolling spasms rocked her time and time again.

'Yes…' he murmured around her flesh, nibbling at her tortured nipple with firm lips and licks of fire from the gentle scrape of his teeth. 'Give me more, Olivia. Give me everything.'

He kept up the suction, carrying her past the molten liquid phase until the sharp bite of arousal gripped her once more. Sweat gathered at Alex's hairline. He shifted, stretching her hands above her head and raising himself up on his knees to deepen the penetration. His smooth gliding thrusts picked up tempo, jerking to pound her sex with the wildness she'd craved.

His teeth gripped his bottom lip as he fought for his own pleasure. She wanted to push him over, as he'd pushed her. She longed to give him what she knew he wanted. Some promise. Some commitment. Some acknowledgment that what they had between them was as unique for her as he'd hinted it was for him.

She wriggled her hands free of his, reaching between them to cup his face. He twisted his head, his

lips kissing the centre of one palm before he sought her
eyes once more.

Muscles bulged in his jaw. His face contorted as his
hips grew more frantic. 'Come with me, Libby.'

She gripped his face tighter, her stare seeking deep
inside his. "Alex… I…'

He roared, his face twisted with rapture as he came,
grasping her shoulders and giving her a third orgasm as
surely as he'd given her a part of himself.

Libby pressed her toes into the soft sand. The tiny
grains reflected the glint of a perfect Mediterranean
morning. This early, they practically had the strip of
golden beach to themselves, the only sounds the oc-
casional cry of a gull and the constant drone of jet ski
engines.

She lifted one hand to shield her eyes, catching a
glimpse of Alex streaking ahead of Jack as they traversed the bay, plumes of water in their wakes. Her
stomach lurched, and the familiar jolt of adrenaline
was one of the reasons she'd opted for sunbathing over
skimming the surface of the Med on little more than a
bicycle with a propeller.

She flopped back onto her lounger, closing her eyes
and forcing herself to think of something other than
death or permanent injury. Only one thought emerged—
Alex. Opening up to him last night had left her palms
damp and her mouth dry. But she couldn't bring herself
to regret it for one second. They'd fallen asleep covered
in each other, as close as two people could be. Breathing

the same air, skin touching from head to toe, sharing soft, sleepy kisses until unconsciousness claimed them.

It changed nothing. This time tomorrow she'd be on a flight back to New York. But something inside her had renewed. A hard kernel had cracked open and the tiny green shoot inside, delicate but brave, was pushing into the sunlight. She'd developed feelings for him. In the space of a few short days. A cliché. A whirlwind. Completely blindsiding her.

Now what? Pining over the changes to her working relationship with Sonya, reeling from her conflicted emotions, living a whole continent away? The obstacles seemed greater than ever. And Alex hadn't verbalised his feelings beyond stating that he wanted to see her again. Perhaps he'd meant once a year, when he travelled to New York on business.

And the reasons for her reluctance still simmered inside her. When he'd winked and suggested she ride pillion with him on the jet ski she'd shrunk away, feigning a desire to work on her tan rather than confess the truth.

She'd been there. Once was enough. If she'd been riding the motorbike that day, been in control, would the outcome have differed? Would she be married to Callum now? About to celebrate their three-year anniversary? Pregnant with his baby?

The daydreams left her skin prickled with goosebumps. She rubbed her arms, trying and failing to rub the unsettling thoughts from her mind. If she'd had all of that she wouldn't be here now, with Alex. She wouldn't know that his eyes sparked when he teased her, that he danced when he was happy and didn't care if anyone

saw him, or that on the mornings they awoke together
he'd pad to the kitchen dressed only in boxers to make
her a 'proper cup of English tea'.

The angry roar of an engine grabbed Libby from
her reverie. She sat up in time to see Alex, his jet ski
aimed at an oncoming wave, travelling at full throttle.

What the hell?

Libby's stomach lurched into her throat. Her hand
covered her mouth as his jet ski hit the wave head-on.
The wall of water tossed the small craft into the air,
flipping it upside down, and the hollow growl of the
airborne engine ricocheted inside Libby's skull until
her eardrums threatened to perforate.

Her mind blanked. Her body tensed on the very edge
of the lounger while time slowed and Alex seemed sus-
pended in mid-air for what felt like a year. And then,
with a slap as it hit the surface, the jet ski righted itself,
the somersault complete, and Alex raced over to Jack,
hand raised with a fist-pump of victory.

Icy shivers covered Libby's body. Every hair rose to
attention. Every muscle twitched. As her stomach settled back inside her abdomen where it belonged, allowing air inside her lungs, the epiphany struck.

She loved him.

She'd fallen in love with an adrenaline junkie. A man
not content just to enjoy the thrill, but who wanted to
push the boundaries to the limit. A limit that made her
hands tremble and her vision darken.

Libby reeled. She had to move. To do something with
the restless energy boiling inside her.

She reached for her sarong, slipping it on and gathering up her phone and a set of keys for one of the estate's vehicles.

Before she'd taken two steps she snapped her head round as another guttural roar cut through the warm air. Libby froze. Her feet stuck to the hot sand. Her eyes were glued to the unfolding drama.

This somersault was higher, its angle, even to Libby's untrained eye, more acute, and the wave to which Alex trusted his life bigger. As he disappeared from view over the crest Libby took off running.

Her legs acted independently of her mind, her ears trained for the landing slap. It came, but the wave continued to roll ashore, obscuring her view. Had he made it? Was he unconscious? Bleeding? His lungs full of seawater?

The wave broke and the orange hull of the capsized jet ski flashed. Her eyes scanned the water, her knees almost buckling when Alex surfaced, his arm raised with a wave to let them know he was okay. Within seconds Jack had cruised over to his cousin, the jet ski was righted and Alex had climbed back into the driver's seat.

But Libby was done.

She'd seen enough to last her two lifetimes. The ice in her blood boiled. If he came in now she wouldn't be responsible for the things she said. Changing direction, she hurried up the beach, the heat on her back and under her feet adding to the fury and impotence raging inside her.

She needed time to think. She needed distance.

Everything between them had happened so quickly, and now her feelings for Alex were spiralling out of control. She'd vowed after Callum's funeral never to get this close again. But here she was, in love with a daredevil billionaire with a penchant for fast toys and dangerous sports. *No.* She couldn't do it again. Refused to put herself through it.

She'd loved Callum. She loved Alex. It terrified her to admit it, but if she didn't she'd make the mistake of being led by her feelings, of succumbing to their insidious allure.

She arrived at one of the vehicles, her hand trembling on the automatic lock. Alex and Jack would have the truck and trailer, so they could get back to the château in time for the wedding. But she had to get away.

If she had to watch Alex do that again... *No.*

She gunned the engine. She didn't know the way back, but the car was top of the range and fitted with GPS. And right now, with all the turmoil pounding through her, getting lost for a few hours wasn't such a bad idea.

She didn't want Alex to worry about her when he discovered her missing, so she plugged her phone into the hands-free and set off. He'd call when he came ashore and she'd text him when she'd calmed down.

She drove, the twisting coastal road that hugged the cliffs a perfect distraction from her riotous thoughts. Halfway back to the château a call came in. But it was Vinnie's voice that startled her.

'Libby? Sonya's been admitted to hospital. I thought you should know.'

Stunned, Libby indicated and pulled off the road, killing the engine. 'What's wrong?'

'All's well, but her blood pressure is high. They'll be inducing labour in the morning.'

She pressed her forefinger to her throbbing temple, her mind flying between thinking of all the necessary arrangements and concern for her friend and her un-born child.

'Change my flight, Vinnie.'

'Sonya said to tell you she's fine. It's just a precaution because she's at term.'

Libby used a tone he'd understand. 'Get me on the next flight home.'

A pause. Then, 'Sure.'

She hung up and pulled back onto the road, break-ing a few French traffic laws.

Yes, she probably had time to wait for Alex to re-turn, to explain why she'd left him at the beach and why she was leaving France earlier than she'd planned. But, whether she'd asked or not, Sonya needed her. And would voicing her views on Alex's reckless behaviour change anything? Did she even *want* to change him? The problem was hers.

She swallowed, her throat hot and her eyes stinging. Cowardice won. She chose to run.

CHAPTER TWELVE

ALEX SHIFTED IN the seat as he waited for the call to connect, the creak of leather as irritating as the view of the cumulus through the tiny window of his jet. The brief journey to London crawled, every second drawn out to breaking point. How could he have been so stupid?

When he'd found Libby gone after returning to the beach yesterday he'd feared every scenario but the truth—kidnapping, murder, drowning—as if his mind hadn't wanted to believe the obvious. He'd messed up and she was gone.

He scrubbed his knuckles down the side of his face, the rasp of stubble evidence of his hasty departure from France that morning. He'd have left last night if it hadn't been for his cousin's wedding. He'd missed most of the nuptials anyway, with his mind going over every second of his time with Libby and every word of their conversations.

The call connected.

'Mr Lancaster,' said Molly. 'I'm sorry. I was in the shower.'

Fuck. He had no excuse for behaving like a shitty boss today. He'd make it up to her.

'Can you schedule an appointment for me with Libby Noble at her New York office at her earliest convenience, please, Molly? And send flowers to Sonya Pullman via the Noble and Pullman offices.'

He understood that Libby would be worried for her friend. Of course she'd want to rush to her side. But without saying goodbye? Without any discussion on the state of their relationship?

The final words of her brief explanatory text replayed in his head, over and over, mocking him with their finality.

Sorry to have to say goodbye via text. Thank you for a wonderful week. I'll always remember it. Good luck with the charity, and if you're ever in New York... Libby xx

His fist clenched hard around the phone. 'I'll be on the ground in twenty minutes. Can you have an overnight bag delivered to the airport and make the necessary arrangements? I'll be flying straight to New York after refuelling.'

He'd tried the personal approach, calling and then texting Libby. He didn't blame her for her silence.

He'd enticed her to be his date at a wedding—likely a trigger for her, given that she must have cancelled her own wedding whilst grieving and burying her fiancé.

He'd drawn out her perfect sublime surrender to him, with their lovemaking opening up new trust, a deeper connection, unspoken endearments.

And then he'd spooked her, no doubt forcing her to relive the worst moment of her life, with his jet ski stunts.

He'd known her reticence as soon as she'd declined to ride behind him. Part of him had wanted to forgo the rush of skimming the bay. But he'd also wanted to demonstrate his competence. Not showing off, but showing Libby that life was for living. The somersault—something he'd perfected from the age of sixteen—had been a step too far.

He pinched the bridge of his nose, answering Molly's brief questions with terse, staccato responses. How had he misjudged things so badly? He'd wanted to give Libby a day that would stay in her memory. One that would remind her of their time together. One that would make it impossible for her to deny her feelings. Feelings he guessed terrified her.

He understood her fear. He felt it too. Their brief encounter had rocked him in its intensity. But to walk away? Never to see her again? Never to explore the burgeoning feelings expanding inside him…

He couldn't do it. What he wanted to know was how could *she*? He'd been away from her less than twenty-four hours, but already he ached to see her again, to touch her, to kiss her.

If there was no future beyond their few stolen days she'd have to tell him face to face, in that frank, forthright manner of hers. Tell him that the connection they shared could be easily discarded. Tell him that she was happy simply returning to her safe life, risking nothing—especially her heart.

His PA drew him back to their conversation.

'One last thing, Molly—send a memo to Human Resources to increase your salary by twenty per cent. That's all for now.'

He ended the call, but not before he heard Molly's gasp.

He sagged back into the seat as the pilot announced their descent. He'd always refused to give up without a fight. He had no intention of conceding now. He'd shown Libby he loved her. Now it was time to tell her.

Libby tapped gently at the door of Sonya's private room in the maternity care unit. She peered through the glass, quietly entering when she saw Sonya was awake.

She placed her gifts on a nearby table and went to her friend, pulling her into an embrace that she never wanted to end.

Sonya's tears seeped into the shoulder of Libby's blouse. Libby clung tighter, her mind racing. 'Shh, it's okay.'

Sonya never cried. Not since her first college boyfriend had broken her heart and they'd commiserated with a tub of Ben & Jerry's and two spoons. Libby pulled back, reached for a tissue from the nightstand and wiped her friend's blotchy cheeks.

Sonya gave a tearful chuckle. 'Sorry. I'm told it's the hormones. It had better stop soon or I'm having my tear ducts removed. Rich doesn't know what to do with me,' she said of her husband.

Libby smiled, smoothing the hair back from Sonya's face. 'I'm not sure myself.'

They laughed, breaking the tension, although Libby

was selfishly tempted to add a meltdown of her own.
She'd never felt so adrift.

Swallowing back her own tumult of emotions, she
focussed on her reason for being here. Her friend.

Libby pointed at the Perspex crib on the far side of
the bed, eyes wide. 'Is this her?' she whispered, awe
bubbling up in her chest and her smile making her
cheeks ache.

Sonya nodded, her watery gaze flicking to where
her tiny newborn slept. Libby tiptoed to the crib, her
own throat suspiciously choked. Sonya's daughter had
a shock of black hair, just like her mom. Her tiny fist
was clenched beside her angelic face, which was peace-
ful in slumber.

It was hard for Libby to breathe. She fought the urge
to lift the baby from the crib, bury her face in the soft
down of her hair and sob her heart out.

'She's so beautiful, Son…' Libby stroked the blanket
covering the baby, so as not to wake her.

She mentally shook herself, sucking in a calming
breath. She wasn't prone to ooh-ing and ahh-ing over
babies. She always had her shit together and she never
cried either. She refused to start now. Sonya needed her.

'Amelia,' said Sonya. 'We named her after Rich's
grandmother.

Libby nodded. 'It's beautiful. *She's* beautiful. Well
done, you.' Libby squeezed Sonya's fingers and took
the seat next to her bed, grinning at her friend.

When their smiles had dropped, Libby said, 'What's
with the tube?'

She'd noticed Amelia had a small hollow tube in her mouth, her tiny lips suckling it even in sleep.

Fresh tears gathered on Sonya's lashes. Why had she asked?

'She has a congenital condition.'

Libby hid her shock, passing another tissue to her friend and taking one for herself. Just in case.

'It's called choanal atresia—it means her nasal passages didn't form properly and she can't breathe through her nose.'

Libby scrunched the tissue in her palm. 'Is it serious?'

Her respect for Sonya skyrocketed. Not enough that she'd undergone an emergency C-section to bring her daughter into the world, she now faced further anguish and her tiny newborn might require surgery.

Sonya nodded. 'It's life-threatening. Babies are nose-breathers. She turned blue the first time I tried to nurse her.'

Her sniffs intensified as she tried to continue her story. Libby could only watch and wait, her own eyes burning.

'Most terrified I've ever been in my entire life.' Sonya gripped Libby's fingers tighter. 'She'll need surgery— probably later today or tomorrow.'

Libby reeled. No wonder her fearless friend couldn't stop crying. 'Where's Rich?'

'I sent him to the cafeteria to get some breakfast. He hasn't eaten anything for twenty-four hours.'

Libby dipped her head. 'I'm so sorry. I should have been here sooner.'

Sonya shook her head, her eyes landing on Amelia and softening. 'You couldn't have done anything. It all happened so quickly in the end.'

Libby nodded, at a loss for words. What could she say to comfort her friend? What did she know about what Sonya and Rich were facing? She'd written off having children after Callum died, but the surge of protective instinct crushing her from the inside out gave her a small insight into what they must be feeling.

The women stared at the sleeping baby, turning to face each other with matching indulgent grins on their faces. It was hard not to smile when such incredible beauty existed.

'I love her so much,' said Sonya. 'I didn't realise it would be so...*instantaneous*.'

Libby nodded, a boulder-sized lump lodged in her chest. 'Of course you do. She's perfect.'

Her gaze returned to Amelia, drawn back to the tiny human. For the first time in three years she allowed herself to think, to dream of a future. A future that embraced the kind of love Sonya talked about. The kind of love she felt for Alex.

The moment the plane had left French soil—left *him*—she'd realised her mistake. Every mile that had carried her home had pulled her apart. Rather than providing perspective, as she'd hoped, being back in New York, in her apartment, had merely intensified the jumble of conflicted feelings inside her.

She loved him. She had no idea what to do about it, but she accepted it as truth.

Give me everything, Olivia.

Why hadn't she?

Sonya shifted in the bed, pressing her lips together and clutching her stomach.

Libby startled from her reverie, her hand gripping Sonya's arm.

Her friend breathed out on a slow exhalation. 'I'm fine. Afterpains,' she said in explanation.

As if she hadn't been through enough, there were afterpains? What the hell…?

'Tell me about France.'

No… If she thought about France she'd think about Alex and then the gut-churning would return—that fluttery feeling in her chest that told her she'd made the biggest mistake of her life.

She plastered on a fake smile for Sonya's sake. Her friend had enough on her plate without Libby's self-inflicted dramas. 'I didn't see much of it. Just Nice. It was…*nice*.'

Libby's smile turned genuine. She'd managed to entice a giggle from her friend.

'Beautiful countryside.' She clutched her stomach. 'I ate too much. The French people are delightful, although I couldn't understand a word—'

'What about Alex?' Sonya cut straight to the chase.

She'd known it was coming, that the question was inevitable. They'd been friends for many years. But she wasn't prepared for hearing his name, and the blow winded her as much as Sonya's revelation about Amelia.

She swallowed, psyching herself up to talk about him. 'He…he's fine, I guess.'

Please let him be fine. Better than fine. She must

have pissed him off, rushing out on him the way she had. He'd understand the emergency, but he was smart enough to fill in the blanks. She'd run rather than face him. Face her fear.

'You don't know? You haven't been in touch?' Sonya's brow pinched, her eyes searching.

Libby shrugged. 'I wanted to get back to see you.'

Hot shards pierced Libby's lungs. She'd left him with only a feeble text message in explanation. She'd ignored his calls and texts, telling herself her friend needed her and she could only deal with one life-altering situation at a time.

She looked down at her hands clutched in her lap. 'I was always going to leave.'

Sonya's labour had only sped up Libby's departure. But, oh, how she'd paid the price for her cowardice. Her body was disjointed, her mind flitted aimlessly, unable to settle on one thought, and hateful waves of emotion threatened to break at any second. Would she ever feel normal again? Should she even crave that insipid state? It was so pale in comparison with her wild week with Alex.

She'd never be able to fill her days with enough work, exercise and reading to match the soul-deep contentment she'd found with him. He'd brought her back to life. Not his wealth or his gifts, nor even his enforced adventures. But *him*. The person. The man who gave everything he had to making a difference. The man who'd given her what she needed. The man who'd shown her she could love again.

Sonya had fallen quiet and keenly watchful. Libby

brightened and plastered a smile on her face, but clearly she wasn't quick enough.

Sonya's stare was shrewd. 'Are you seeing him again?'

Libby swallowed. Stalled. She wasn't ready to confess her true feelings for Alex. To anyone. She hadn't had enough time to pick them apart and Sonya would think she was mad, falling for a man she'd only known for a week. Who *did* that?

Fortunately she'd prepared a speech for this eventuality. 'Perhaps. But we both work insane hours and live on different continents, so the chances are slim.' Acid burned her throat. Chances he'd want to see her now were less than slim.

'You don't want to make it work?'

It was a question, but it felt like a statement. Sonya knew her so well. Had been there for her through the dark times. She should have known she'd see right through her and her attempts at nonchalance.

Libby looked at her hands in her lap, her throat tight and her eyes hot. Fatigue made her feel heavy in the chair, the weight of what she'd done pressing her down. She'd had long sleepless hours to make sense of her true feelings—first on the flight from France and then while she paced her apartment, waiting for the sun to come up so she could visit her friend.

Without conscious thought she let the confession tumble out on a whisper, as if the words spoken any louder would have more power over her. Power to hurt.

'I fell in love with him, Son.'

She kept her eyes trained on her fingernails, blind

to everything as she forced air into her lungs. Tried to breathe through a different kind of grief. Not as acute or violent as past pain, but just as devastating.

'Of course you did.'

Sonya was quiet. Libby swallowed, pushing down the overwhelming swell of emotion inside. A tidal wave crashing ashore and destroying every wall she'd built to protect herself over the years.

'You know…' Sonya stroked her hand, drawing her back from the abyss. 'Here's the thing about love…'

Libby swallowed, meeting her friend's sincere gaze.

'We have no choice, do we?' Sonya flicked a glance at her sleeping child, her face aglow with maternal love. 'It's the best emotion and the worst, because it has the power to hurt us like nothing else.'

Libby nodded, her throat too constricted for her to respond.

Sonya's sad smile wobbled on her lips. 'But I wouldn't change it. Not for a second. You don't need me to tell you it's worth it.'

Her eyes burned into Libby's, speaking what she hadn't said aloud. Love was worth the pain. Worth the risk.

Alex was worth loving. Not that she had any choice in the matter.

Libby nodded, lips tight, holding on to her panic, which urged her with every passing second to race to JFK and jump on the first flight back to London.

'If he loves you back,' said Sonya, 'it's not too late. Don't wait. Tell him.'

Both women were startled when the door opened and

Rich entered, his gaze landing first on Sonya, then on his daughter, and finally on Libby.

As if through a fog, she congratulated him and made conversation for a few more minutes. When Sonya tried to hide a yawn she made her excuses and left the new family to themselves, knowing these moments were precious.

Outside the hospital, she hailed a cab. Sonya was right. Alex *was* worth the risk. And she had little choice. She loved him. She could either live a careful life, nursing that love alone, or she could commit to it. Surmount the obstacles, the distance, and love him with her whole being—the way he deserved to be loved. The way *she* deserved.

By the time she entered her office she'd tried his cell phone and his home phone, with no success. His voicemail mocked her. His deep voice a form of aural torture. She'd had a chance at something rare and extraordinary and she'd let it slip away. No. She'd flung it away, as if it had burned. But the pain of her cowardice hurt so much more than the pain of her bravery— especially as she only had herself to blame.

She slammed through the foyer, startling Vinnie, who was in the middle of a call. He hung up, his grin wide, and then let it fall slightly when he saw the expression she clearly couldn't hide.

He stood, rounding the desk with his arms outstretched for a hug. 'Welcome back, hen. Did you have a good trip? Have you seen the wee one? Och, she's a darling. Made me quite broody myself, she did.'

Vinnie always fired multiple questions, as if he already knew the answers.

Libby laughed into his chest, on the verge of sobbing. She accepted the comfort of his hug for an indulgent, unprofessional second.

'Please don't call me hen. I'm not a chicken.'

Vinnie rolled his eyes, this well-worn argument clearly having no effect on him whatsoever. 'You get settled, I'll make you a brew, and then you can tell Uncle Vinnie all about it.'

Her spirits lifted. She could always rely on her outrageous, thick-skinned assistant to cheer her up. She forced her smile into a semiserious scowl. She couldn't let him get away with everything, or he'd run the show.

'I've told you a thousand times. Libby, Ms Noble or even Boss is preferable.' She handed him the small gift she'd bought in London, her throat hot and achy again. Fuck this day and its crazy mood swings. 'Thanks for caring for Sonya and holding the fort.'

He clutched his mouth, his eyes round. 'It isn't…?' He caressed the square package lovingly. 'Scottish? Och, hen, you shouldn't have.'

She laughed and nodded. 'Would I bring you shortbread that wasn't Scottish?'

He hugged her again, his delight infectious. 'You're the best boss in the world, hen.'

Libby rolled her eyes. 'Speaking of which—work to do. First, can you please get Alex Lancaster on the line for me?'

She checked her watch, calculating the time difference. 'He should be still at the office. Speak to Molly, his

PA. He might be at the Able-Active charity. And then you can get me up to speed on everything I've missed—celebrity gossip notwithstanding.'

Vinnie placed his gift in the drawer with reverence. 'I'm on it.'

'And did you send through that list of applicants for Sonya's position?'

He nodded, moving to the coffee machine they kept in the corner, pre-empting her next request.

Her office seemed unfamiliar, disjointed, as if someone had shifted the walls or changed the view through the windows. Had she really only been away a week? So much had changed—her most of all. Now the familiar, the previously comforting, felt like a cage, holding her back.

Distracted, she checked her e-mails, ignoring the fifty or so business-related ones that required her attention before she could leave for the day, her eyes scanning for one from Alex. Nothing. What did that mean? He was over her? He'd accepted her departure without question? He'd moved on?

No. She couldn't allow herself a trip down to that particular mind-trap. Not until she'd spoken to him. Told him how she felt.

With impatient fingers she composed a brief e-mail to him, requesting a phone call. She couldn't put what she had to say in an e-mail. The words were so big she'd break the internet.

Within seconds an automatic response landed in her inbox. Her stomach lurched. Alex Lancaster was out of the office, all requests should be directed to Molly.

What did that mean? Was he still in France? Perhaps he'd moved up that business trip to Japan he'd told her about. Perhaps he'd taken a holiday. Perhaps he wanted nothing to do with her.

Libby straightened her desk, aligning the pens to her left and the pot plant to her right, restless energy bubbling beneath her skin.

Vinnie entered with her coffee. 'No luck with Mr Lancaster, I'm afraid. And I can't get hold of Molly either.' He took one look at her face, placed the coffee on the desk and headed for the door. 'I'll keep trying.'

For the rest of the day she worked in a fog, achieving little, upsetting Vinnie and checking her phone and e-mails every thirty seconds—like a teenager with her first crush. Impotence gripped her, its claws sinking deep until she wanted to climb out of her own skin.

By five, she'd abandoned hope for any constructive work. Her temples throbbed, her eyes were gritty from lack of sleep, and her mind was sluggish with jet lag.

She closed her laptop in disgust, shrugged into her jacket and yelled out to Vinnie, who'd wisely kept a low profile for the last two hours. 'Any news from Sonya? About the surgery?'

'It's scheduled for first thing tomorrow.' His voice boomed back from the outer office through the open adjoining door. He was clearly pissed with her.

Fine. She was pissed with herself. She prided herself on knowing what she wanted professionally. How had she got it so wrong when it came to her personal life?

She stuffed her tablet into her bag and snatched up

her still-silent cell phone, tempted to hurl the useless device through the window.

The time for waiting was over. It was time for action.

She called out to Vinnie again, too impatient to wait the few seconds it would take her to walk to his desk 'Vinnie, book me a flight to London asap.'

What was she thinking? She had work commitments, clients to see, Sonya to support. She couldn't just up and leave again.

But she couldn't sit and do nothing either.

'Ah… Ms Noble,' said Vinnie, his cautious tone carrying through the open door.

Great—now he'd resorted to sarcasm to wind her up. He *never* called her that, despite her constant reprimands.

'I have Alex Lancaster for you.'

Her feet stalled. Her belly flip-flopped. Had she heard him correctly? She reached for the edge of her desk to steady herself.

'Put him through.'

She turned, skirted her desk, dropped into her chair. Her hand hovered over the phone on her desk, her belly rioting. Vinnie mumbled something she didn't catch. Now really wasn't the time for him to have a meltdown. As soon as she'd spoken to Alex she'd apologise to him for her crappy mood today. Promise to take him for lunch tomorrow at his favourite bistro. Buy him a stack of his beloved magazines.

Why wasn't he putting through the call?

She couldn't wait. With a sigh, she strode to the open

door that connected her office to that of her PA. 'Look, I'm sorry. I'll just take the call here.'

She flung open the door.

And came face to face with Alex.

The air left her lungs with a thump. Her stomach recoiled from its temporary location in her throat. Her eyes raked him from head to toe. He was real. He was here. In the flesh.

'Olivia.'

A curt nod. Unreadable eyes. Unsmiling mouth.

But, oh, the scrape of his voice over her strung-out senses was so welcome. Her lungs stuttered back to life, relief pounding through her, quickly followed by thick, syrupy lust. What a sight. Just the way she liked him—nerdy graphic T-shirt, relaxed jeans hugging his hips, his hair an unruly mess that begged for her fingers.

His delicious scent stole all the air from the room. Her mouth dried. Her brain shut down.

'I…'

He's here. Say something.

'How are you?' She flicked her gaze over him. 'What are you doing here?'

Behind Alex, Vinnie was fanning himself, dramatically, his gaze sliding over her man. Libby sheathed her claws. Alex wasn't *her* anything. She'd thrown him away.

'We have unfinished business.' He quirked one brow, his mouth tight, giving nothing away. 'I have a car downstairs. Would you join me so we can discuss it?'

Not frosty, but not friendly either.

He held out his arm, indicating the exit.

Unfinished business? Why was he in New York? For *her*?

She must have performed some jaw-dropping gold-fish impersonation, because Vinnie answered for her.

'She's just finished for the day. She'd love to.'

Jet lag, insomnia and stress—a combination disastrous for her usual quick wit and acidic put-downs.

'I…'

She couldn't even string a sentence together to reprimand her heavy-handed assistant. All she could do was stare. Alex's dark eyes were a magnet.

'Please.'

At last she saw a flicker there—one she'd thought she'd never have a chance to see again.

Hope shocked her brain back to life. Vinnie had her bag in his hand now and was shoving it towards her and urging her to the exit.

'I'll finish up here, boss.' He gave her a wink.

She'd absolutely have to fire him. Tomorrow.

She made the short journey outside on seriously wobbly legs. Alex, at her side, kept his hands to himself and Libby wasn't sure whether to weep or climb over him and remind him how good they were together.

Then she remembered the way she'd left him. Her fingers flexed. She craved the feel of him, but could she face his rejection? Had she broken their connection permanently?

On the street, Alex ushered her inside the waiting car, following her inside and taking the seat opposite. The car pulled away from the kerb, entering the stream of evening traffic.

She looked at him. For the first time free of the shock of seeing him here. The noises of the outside world vanished. Her mind cleared. They stared across the chasm separating them.

Her eyes drank him in, cataloguing every minute detail of his beloved face. The smudged circles beneath his dark eyes, the day's worth of stubble covering his jaw, the muscle ticking there. Perhaps he'd had as little sleep as her over the last twenty-four hours.

His voice, when it came, washed over her, alerting every nerve ending with its low rumble.

'You didn't say goodbye.'

His eyes were piercing, pinning her to the leather. Shame forced her to glance away. 'I… I did.'

He shook his head. 'Not in person.'

Her throat closed. 'No.'

I love you.

Why was this so hard? Would he think her mad? He'd only asked to see her again. Why was her mind, currently struggling to think of *anything*, overthink this?

'Why?'

Good question. She met his stare again, heat blooming in her belly. 'I'm a coward.'

Nothing.

'I'm scared, Alex.' The words fled in a rush.

A single nod and then he stayed silent, giving her the space she needed, time to turn the jumble in her head into words.

'I've been scared for so long I've forgotten how to be anything else.' Libby focussed on his eyes, their unique beauty a lifeline. Perhaps she could say what she had to say. She needed him to understand why she'd messed up so monumentally.

'I held Callum in my arms that day I lost him. I watched the life drain out of him—watched the vibrant man I loved fade away.' She stared harder, willing him to comprehend. Willing him to give her another chance. 'I never want to go through that again.' Her voice broke.

He swallowed, his eyes glittering chips of amber. Still silent.

She reached for his hand, almost sagging to the floor when his fingers squeezed hers. 'I thought I couldn't love again. But I can. Because I love you. And it terrifies me.'

Air gusted out of him, his shoulders sagging. 'Thank fuck.'

He reached for her other hand, tugging her to the edge of the seat. A small smile lifted the corners of his mouth and his gaze wandered her features as he cupped her face between his palms.

'Because I love you, too, Libby. I followed you to tell you.' His thumbs swiped at her cheeks. 'I should have told you in France.'

He stared with so much heat, so much passion, Libby expected her skin to scorch. It had been there all along, this searing connection. She'd just chosen to ignore it. For her sanity. Had taken the coward's way out.

Covering his hand with hers, she pressed his palm to her cheek, turning her head to place a kiss at its centre while her chest inched ever closer to exploding.

'Short of begging you to love me back, I only had one other strategy.'

She pressed her lips together, holding in a smile at the playful twist of his mouth and lifting her eyebrows. 'And that was…?'

He shrugged, a wicked spark flashing in his eyes. 'Fucking you into submission.'

A laugh burst from her, her tension dissipating. She went to him. She'd been away from him for too long. Had missed touching him, kissing him. Holding him. He caught her, strong arms banded around her back as she pushed him into the seat and straddled his lap.

He cupped her waist with one arm, holding her close. 'Libby…'

Her mouth touched his and the fire reignited, flaring to life from the smouldering embers they'd left behind in France.

She kissed him and giggled and spoke at the same time. 'Well, that sounds fun.'

She tunnelled her fingers into his hair, twisting them until his head dropped back on the seat behind him, and then she raised herself over him, deepening the kiss when his lips opened to welcome her.

Then he shook his head, pulling away, his face serious. 'No. There'll be no more fucking.'

Libby shuffled back. His hand gripped her, preventing her retreating completely.

He gazed up at her, eyes brimming with love. 'From now on we'll be making love.'

He cupped the back of her neck, bringing her close for another kiss.

She laughed, breaking away to pepper kisses on his

forehead, his cheeks and his closed eyes, loving the groan she pulled from him.

He joined her, punctuating each frantic kiss with words. 'Hard...' *kiss* '...greedy...' *kiss* '...fast or slow...' *kiss*. 'However you want it.'

She smiled, kissing him back, keen to get started on all that loving. Then she sobered, glancing out of the window.

'Where are we going?'

She climbed from his lap, settling beside him and holding on tight to his hand in case he disappeared.

He stared at her as if he couldn't believe she was real. She knew the feeling. The comfort of his warm hand in hers was the only thing convincing her he was there.

'Well, as you live here I was hoping you'd invite me to your apartment so we can make a start on that love-making.'

He smacked his lips together, eyes glittering as he leaned closer.

'Perhaps we could begin with some good, old-fashioned show and tell?'

His accent grew haughtier, and the disparity between his cultured tone and the searing look in his eyes was enough to make her hot and achy.

'You know how much I enjoy that. And it's a particular skill of yours.' He arched a brow, one finger tracing the top button of her blouse.

She grinned, remembering the torture she'd inflicted on him that first time. 'Good plan.'

Her cheeks twitched, aching with the effort of holding in so much euphoria.

He nodded, a self-satisfied smirk on his face. 'Otherwise we could go to the apartment I've just bought here.'

He flopped back into the luxuriant seat, tugging her onto his lap once more.

'You're joking?'

She tried to think while his lips explored the base of her throat with nibbling kisses. He lived in England. Why purchase an apartment where he'd only spend a few weeks a year?

'I never joke about business, Ms Noble.' He tugged on her earlobe with his lips, his words almost whispered. 'I'll be spending considerable time here in New York. I have a new business venture I'm exploring.'

'You do?'

He pulled back, his stare earnest. He gave a nod.

'And you're the best deal I've ever negotiated.'

* * * * *

LET'S TALK
Romance

For exclusive extracts, competitions
and special offers, find us online: